# THE SERUM

RUTH A. MILLIGAN

# CHAPTER ONE

Alarms illuminated white hallways with crimson lights as the high-pitched squeal echoed throughout the Juniper Ridge mutant hospital. The piercing warning consumed the building, the mutants howling and cawing at high decibels.

Doctor Sven Olander covered his ears. "Good Lord, not another one. There's no way a man can work through all this commotion."

He huffed at the security monitor next to his desk, the screen a snowy white of static that matched the white in his hair. Abandoning his notes, he slammed the door of his office and rushed down the hall, his lab coat flying behind him. Slipping as he turned a corner, he caught himself. At seventy-two-years-old, his body wasn't what it once was. He took the elevator to the floor beneath him and peered down at the source of the cacophony.

Security, a tall, well-built man in his early twenties, stood at the lab's entrance. Broken glass from inside the room rang in Sven's ears. "That better be equipment!" Sven shouted between gasps, working through the gawkers in his way. He knew it was more than equipment with the coppery, sweet smell of the serum. "Tom, what is going on here?" Sven leaned forward and put his hands on his knees, catching his breath. "We need to get every bit of that serum off the floor. Do you hear me?"

"Yes, sir," said Tom, tucking his head down, "but I'm just out here making sure no one else goes through." Sven gave him a hard stare as he regained his breath before his expression softened. Sven patted him on the shoulder. "Dr. Olander is out here asking questions." Tom stepped aside so Sven could see what was happening.

"Busy here," a voice came from inside. The security guards held down a young woman no older than twenty, her dark nest of hair flying everywhere. She jerked beneath them, almost biting one as he moved his arm out of the way. Her eyes were so dilated and bloodshot, they appeared to be on fire.

"Let me go!" she screamed at the top of her lungs. "I will listen to you if you just let me go!"

"No way," said one of them, and the other agreed. "Not until the authorities arrive."

"How the hell did she get in here, anyway?" asked Sven to Tom. "With all the added security, you would think the lack of windows in the building would make a difference."

"That serum," said Tom. "They always find a way." Even with the code to get through the gate, the badge, and the retinal scans, they still got inside. Behind him, more hurried footsteps rang down the hallway.

"Sven, are you okay?" Adam Davidson leaned down to be eye to eye with Sven in his crouched position, his long, slender fingers resting on his knees for balance.

"Fine, I ran," he sputtered between breaths. "I just wanted to make sure..."

"I heard the alarms," said Jesse Stein, coming up on the other side of the open door. "But there was all that broken glass. Hey, do you two need any help?" While Jesse was wearing lab coats like the rest of his colleagues, his muscular form underneath made him appear more like one of the security guards. Before waiting for a reply, Jesse shoved his way into the room.

The security guards both yelled no, even though Jesse continued moving toward the chaos as two cops entered the hallway. The pounding of their boots echoed on the crisp tiles that they muddied from the pouring rain. One stood tall and thin with large ears, the other stocky and tough. The tough one burst through the crowd and cuffed the girl in one swift motion. She kicked and screamed, so he slammed her against the wall while his partner read her rights to her in a booming, deep voice.

"Are you guys okay?" the cop with the cuffs asked the security guards as he held the thief against the wall. "I will have to take statements from you. Come on into the station and we'll take care of it."

"Break it up!" said the other cop to the onlookers as they rushed back to work. Janitors, doctors, nurses, and administrative personnel scattered back to their workspaces once again. The cops and the intruder went to leave when Adam glanced at the floor of the lab.

Broken beakers of a light green substance covered the ground, the glass mixed in with the medicine. The serum.

"Oh, shortcake," Adam said, moving closer. He closed the door on the refrigerator that held more of the potent item. He ran his fingers through his short, onyx hair. "There's a lot wasted here."

"Shortcake?" asked Jesse.

"Camille has been repeating what I say," explained Adam, referring to his eight-year-old daughter. "I'm trying to keep the cussing down."

"Good luck with that," said Jesse.

"Thank God we have more serum in other parts of the hospital. It will be better when we can finally finish everything set up underneath this place to hold the bulk of it. It's almost impossible to get down there unless you really know your way around," said Adam.

Sighing, Jesse shook his head. "I'll stay and clean it up. Maybe I can save some of it."

"There's no way," argued Adam. "We're just going to deal with what we have until we can make more. It's contaminated. We can't use this."

"You know I'm right." Jesse's hands tightened into fists as his stance spread. "I'll handle the problem myself. I'm not a wimp like last year. Do you remember I stopped Jill?" spat Jesse.

"That's not the point." Adam's voice remained steady and calming.

Sven knelt and stared at the wasted serum. As if staring at it long enough, it would magically be back in its rightful place in the refrigerator.

"But we need this now," said Jesse. "We are short enough as it is."

Adam knelt down to where Sven was looking and abandoned the argument. "Maybe you should sit down, Sven. You don't look well."

Jesse knelt as well, and they both helped Sven stand up again. Light-headed and tired, his mind drifted, and he yearned for sleep, which wouldn't happen unless he had answers. "Oh, I'll be fine." He continued to stare at the ground. "God damn it, what difference does it make, anyway?" *Circles, we are moving in circles. It's getting better, but it is taking so long.*

Thirty-five years ago, a virus had spread through the water supply, devastating the planet and causing dangerous mutations in both humans and animals alike. Treated at Juniper Ridge under experimental conditions, the scientists were making inconsistent progress until Adam found a cure, a tree frog, which they thought was extinct. Tree frogs were the only animals that were immune to the mutant virus, and in its blood, held the cure.

Now that cure was all over the laboratory floor.

"It looks like you could use some rest," said Jesse. "Why don't you go home and I can take it from here?"

"I don't want to go home. We have things we need to do here. I won't stay late tonight."

"Promise?" asked Adam.

"Yes," said Sven. *Geez, you would think they were my elders, not the other way around.*

Adam found some chemical cleaner and Jesse sang a recent heavy-metal tune under his breath as he helped him clean up the mess. "I don't know who thought of using this for recreational drug use in the first place," said Adam. "I should have kept it quiet. If we kept it under wraps..."

"No," said Sven. "Then we wouldn't have been able to help all the people that we have. This is not your fault."

"He's right," Jesse added. "None of this is your fault. It's not like the public knows how rare it is. Why someone would want to hallucinate is beyond me. The world is crazy enough."

"I guess you're right," agreed Adam.

"At least things are getting better," said Sven. "Fixing it won't be a quick process. As long as we are going in the right direction."

Adam made a shutter. "I guess I'm glad Camille isn't older, or she might get caught up in the craze."

"Camille is smarter than that," said Jesse. "I'll gather up what I can…"

"Dispose of it in the waste barrels," said Sven. "There's no way we can use this. Adam's right."

"Fine," said Jesse, rolling his eyes. Sven wondered if Jesse would really do what he said with the care he took to gather it back in an empty container. "I should get back to my rounds. We now have mutants and serum junkies to see. Would either of you like to join me?"

Sven straightened up as he cleared his throat. "As long as they are our patients and you wear that lab coat, Dr. Stein, they are drug abusers, not junkies."

Jesse opened his mouth, then shut it.

"I thought so. I still have things to do," said Sven. "Looking over some research notes and figuring out how all the patients are reacting to the serum. Why don't you stop by and let me know how things are progressing? I should be here for a little while longer."

Jesse nodded.

"I'll join you," said Adam. "I just have a few other patients to check on, and I will be right with you. I'm running ahead, anyway."

Sven's phone pulsed around his wrist. Holding up his finger in a one-moment gesture, the voice on the other end of the line made his heart jump. "Dr. Olander, you need to get home as fast as you can."

"Thank you." He hung up, his exhaustion and anxiety over the serum forgotten. "It's Hannah's nurse," he explained to Adam and Jesse, making the rush to the serum look like a leisurely stroll. "And it's not good. I have to get home."

# CHAPTER TWO

S ven crept up to Hannah's bedside, a hospital bed that he had set up in their bedroom when her lung cancer worsened. Watching her nurse adjust her pillow after Hannah's head hung at a strange angle, he said, "Thank you, Brenda, for calling me, and for taking such good care of her."

The older woman smiled, putting her hand on his. "Of course." Brenda pointed to the pill container on the nightstand. "Her final pill is all ready, to make her more comfortable and I can stay to give it to her myself, unless you want to."

"I'll do it." *For better or worse. I'm her husband and I will do it.* "Thank you again. If I need anything, I know the number."

He knew that normally the nurse would stay, take all the vitals, note the time of death, but since he was a doctor, these were all things he could take care of. Pulling up a chair, the worn cryonics brochure fell off the nightstand that crumpled under his foot. Grasping her thin, icy hand, he pressed it to his cheek. "Dear Hannah." Her eyes remained closed, and her breathing was shallow.

The images came unbidden; her walking down the aisle on their wedding day, pink flowers woven in her chestnut brown hair that matched the pink of her lipstick. Her smile that flashed a dimple in her left cheek took his breath away, that day and all the days after.

For a second, he wondered if she knew he was sitting next to her bed.

But she knew.

She opened her eyes, staring at the ceiling. Her breathing quickened, then stopped. Sven put his head to her chest, gingerly so as not to break her, and sighed when he heard the heartbeat. It was faint, but it was still there.

"I love you," he said. "You and me against the world. So happy." He kissed her lips. "I'm not ready to let you go. I know I should, but I don't think I will ever be ready. Life is unimaginable without you." He listened to her rushed breathing, stared at her blank expression, and held her hand tight again. "I'm sorry."

On top of the nightstand, in a red container the size of a small vial, held a dissolvable pill. The final pill that would make her feel more comfortable in her last moments. He thought of all the years that she was ill, struggling to breathe on her own, and how helpless he felt to help her.

He pulled back her lip and tucked the pill between her cheek and gums. Lips moistened with a swab, he said, "I wish I could keep you here with me, but don't hold on any longer, my love. I don't want you to suffer. Not for me. I will see you someday and the world will be different. I promise." Sven gazed out the barred windows they had installed years ago for added protection, and he remembered when they first got together. No bars. They walked the streets carefree. The world was so different back then. His gaze moved back to her face. No smog polluted the air, the weather was gorgeous, and the water was pure before they found the virus in it. Now was the time to fix everything to return to the days when there were no mutants.

Sven reached down to push a button on her bed that began the cooling process immediately after death, not wanting to take any chances of his plan being ruined. His watch rang, but it was a background noise to him, his gaze unmoving from Hannah's face. Her long, white hair fanned around her face like a halo. The wrinkles in her face deepened and her pale skin turned almost ghostlike. She had changed a lot over the years, but those big, brown doe eyes never changed.

"How is she?" asked Adam.

Sven jumped, realizing that he must have tapped his wrist by habit. Saying nothing back, his throat was like sandpaper and his gut was in knots. He wondered how Adam knew, and then he remembered Adam was there when he got the call.

"I'll be there as soon as I can," said Adam.

He could hear Jesse in the background. "We're going to have to get going."

"Five minutes," said Adam, and the watch clicked.

Sven remembered the first time she met Adam and Hannah offered him homemade peanut butter cookies. Adam's face when she pulled out the scotch and poured herself that enormous glass. Sven laughed. "Hannah, I am going to miss you so much." Breathing became difficult as his lungs tightened. Sven fought back tears, refusing to cry. This wasn't forever and he wouldn't admit that this was it.

The doorbell rang, and he hit the button on his watch to unlock it. "Come on in," he said into his watch, which was connected to a speaker by the entrance. A man and a woman entered the room, the woman tall and thin, the man short with wide shoulders. "Oh," he said, "I didn't realize it was you. You're here early. I'm not ready yet."

"It's okay, Mr. Olander," said the man, putting his hand on Sven's shoulder. "You take all the time you need."

"We just wanted to be here as quickly as possible. The sooner we can start the freezing procedure after death, the better," said the woman, so matter of fact, he wanted to slap her.

"It already began." Sven patted the side of the bed that read Cole's, the same company that was embroidered on their shirts.

"My apologies. I didn't realize you purchased one of our cooling pre-chamber beds." He kept his focus on Hannah. The woman was just doing her job and helping him. Keep everything in perspective, he told himself. This won't be forever. The man nudged her, and she straightened. "I'm sorry for your loss. You just let us know when you are ready."

"I love you, Hannah." A rock formed in his lungs as he fought the urge to cry. She won't be gone forever, and he refused to surrender to that idea. This wasn't the way he wanted her to remember him before her return. He smiled with a squeeze of her hand. He remembered the first moment he saw her. They were in the grocery store. She was the woman that worked in the deli, and before she started, he went grocery shopping every two weeks. The strangest thing happened. Suddenly, he would crave cold cuts daily. After he had tried all the cheese and meats that they offered, he asked her out on a date. His refrigerator was getting too full and his patience was too thin.

And she said yes.

He remembered the first time Hannah came over and he went to take the cheese platter out of the fridge, and she saw his grand array of cheese. That sweet laughter is a sound he would never forget. Then she admitted she would have gone out with him after he bought the Provolone. Laughing, he said, "You didn't know yet that I hate Provolone."

He couldn't take the silence as his laughter subsided. Sven was determined to remember the good times and reject the idea that this was forever. "Remember when I put that fake snake in the kitchen cabinet? I apologize for that one. In my defense, I didn't know you had a fear of snakes. I learned quickly, didn't I? I guess I've always enjoyed a good prank every so often, but after that, no snakes."

Her breathing slowed even more, her chest barely rising. The wheezing was faint, and he put his stethoscope in his ears, placing the end over her precious heart. Sven leaned over and kissed her forehead.

5:05 P.M. She was gone.

The doorbell rang again, and he let Jesse and Adam in. They rushed into the back of the house, stopping at the open door. Adam reached out to Sven and hugged him without a word. "I'm here for you," Adam said after Sven pulled away. Sven reached out for him again, just for a moment.

"We both are," said Jesse, who hugged Sven.

Sven looked down at his wife, then asked the men, "Did you want to say goodbye?"

Adam stood next to her, then sat down where Sven was before. "Hannah, you were my friend, and I am glad I got to know you. The indoor picnics wouldn't have been the same without your stories or your cherry pie. Don't worry about Sven. We are all going to be here for him." Adam kissed her on the forehead and moved aside.

Jesse's eyes were bloodshot from crying as he looked down at Hannah, the tears streaming down his cheeks once more. "I…" Jesse stared down at her, unable to speak.

Sven looked at his two friends and realized how lucky he was. "She knows, Jesse. You don't have to say a thing."

Jesse bobbed his head in acknowledgment.

"I guess she's ready," said Sven to the two professionals. "I will be by shortly to sign all the paperwork."

"Take your time," said the woman.

Sven turned away, looking out the window to the overcast day, watching the birds flying near the nest that was accumulating in the tree. He couldn't watch them take her away. He could feel Adam's hand on his shoulder.

"Now I need to go. There's something I need to take care of," said Sven.

"You're not driving anywhere. We will take you anywhere you need to go," said Jesse. "Where to?"

"I need to make sure they are taking good care of my Hannah."

— · —

# CHAPTER THREE

"Here?" Jesse pulled his jeep into the parking lot after Sven gave him the directions. "You brought Hannah here? A Cryonic company?"

"I thought we were going to a funeral home," said Adam from the back seat. "You know that makes more sense."

Sven stiffened. *I knew they wouldn't understand. I should have just come myself after they left. But they offered.* The thought of being alone made him shiver. He flipped backwards to face Adam and said, "Yes, because if there is even a sliver of a chance to bring her back, you don't think that I would do it?"

Adam's voice softened. "I hate to say it, but you know that none of this works. You are a scientist and you know you can't freeze someone and bring them back. We work in science, not science fiction."

"You don't have to go in with me. I wouldn't expect either of you to understand. Losing a parent isn't like losing a wife. She is my life." He got out of the jeep, slamming the door. Tension took over his whole body. *They don't know what it's like to be married to someone for fifty-three years and have that all taken away in an instant. To look into someone's eyes and see the lights go out.*

"Wait!" yelled Jesse, crawling out of the jeep, Adam right behind him.

"I'm sorry," said Adam. "Doing this isn't healthy." He placed his hand on Sven's shoulder. "You need to accept the fact that she's gone and mourn. We are both here for you. I'm just trying to help."

Sven shook away his hand. "Well, you aren't."

"We're trying, Sven, and Adam is right." Jesse looked at them both urgently. "We better get in that facility or back in the car. I hate to bring it up, but there are still mutants on the rise again with the serum shortage." Jesse's eyes darted around the area. The air grew increasingly cold, and the clouds were gathering more than before. Rain fell. Adam and Jesse followed Sven into the building.

Sven thought of Adam's wife and two children, his face scowling with envy. He hated it. He loved Adam's family, and those kids were like grandchildren to him. But they weren't his grandchildren, not really.

The reception area was simple and clean. Two couches were on one side, making an L, joined by a plastic tree. Hardback chairs were on the other side, lined in a row against the wall. A deep oak counter was in the middle of the seating areas, separated by sections. Three receptionists stood behind the counter.

Two were working on their computers, and the other one greeted them both with a smile. She had hot pink hair flowing down to her waist, and a gold metal ball pierced her right eyebrow.

"How can I help you gentlemen?" she asked.

"My name is Sven Olander. My wife just arrived here," he said.

"Her name?" As Sven gave her the information, she typed it in the computer and he handed over the rest of his fee with his credit card: twenty thousand dollars. She then led the three men to a room to wait.

"How long do you plan on keeping her here?" asked Jesse.

"Until I can figure a way to bring her back to me. Don't worry, I have a backup plan." He was growing tired of explaining his actions. A headache was beginning right behind his left eye and nausea hit him.

Leaning forward to catch his breath, Adam apologized. "I'm sorry, Sven."

Waiting for over thirty minutes, they entered another room with light gray walls and cylinders lined up about two feet apart from the wall. The cylinders were twelve feet tall, three feet in circumference, and misty like frosted glass from a chilly day. They echoed a low hiss. Beyond the glass, outlines of bodies stood straight upright. Three rows of eighteen cylinders filled the cool room. Sven shivered.

"Where is my wife?" he asked the man that had led him there. Aside from his lab coat, he looked nothing like a doctor. His bug eyes were bigger from his coke-bottle glasses, and acne covered his face. So young.

"This one." Matt, the boy said, pointing to the third one from the end. Sven pointed to the empty cylinder next to Hannah's. "Yes, and we got your deposit for that one as well, just as you requested."

*They sure set her up quickly, but that was what they had to do. To make it work.* Sven placed his hand on the outside of the cylinder, and he saw her silhouette through the misted glass.

"You will come back to me," he said to her. He thought of them living in the new world, where the mutants were gone, where they were all free, and they would be so happy. Like before, but better. Her poor lungs wouldn't hurt anymore and she could breathe freely.

Sven did not know how long he had been standing there until Matt said, "I'm sorry, Mr. Olander, but I have many other things to attend to. If you would like to come back at another time..."

"Now listen..." started Adam, but Sven reached out and touched his arm to stop him.

"That's fine. I'm tired anyway. I think I need to go home and lie down," said Sven.

"I will just need you to sign some paperwork." Matt's wrist phone rang. "If you will excuse me for a moment." He walked away into the next room and closed the door.

"Okay, Sven, I am assuming the other spot is for you?" asked Jesse.

"Of course." Both of the men were quiet, which worried Sven more than if they were yelling at him. "What will happen if we find a cure for everything right after I have a heart attack or get killed by a mutant? I need both of you to promise after I'm gone, if I'm not with Hannah, that you will follow through. You will bring us back when the time comes." He paused, taking a deep breath. "And that is my backup plan."

"Sven…" started Adam, but Jesse interrupted him.

"Nothing is going to happen to you." Jesse took a step toward Sven, putting his hand on his shoulder. "You know I'm right."

"Now, Jesse," Adam said, "he has a point."

"You're on board with all of this? What happened to this all being science fiction? Cryonics hasn't changed in decades, so how is it going to help her now?" He took a step back from Sven. "I'm sorry, Sven, but Hannah is gone. You are here, now, and you have to concentrate on yourself and your own health."

"You want to know my plan and how it's going to all work out?" They were quiet, listening. "My second backup plan? If I don't bring her back by the end of the year, I am going to end my life and join her at the facility. I will not have her return to find out something happened to me, and I will not live without her longer than that. I refuse."

A full minute of silence passed.

"But, Sven…" started Adam. "That's only two months."

"Quiet. I just want to go home and have time to myself."

"I'm worried about you," said Adam.

"I love Hannah more than anyone," said Sven. "And that's what matters."

Alarms of consistent bells blared through the hallways, the lights flickering. All three scientists crouched down in a defensive stance, aware of their surroundings. Matt emerged from the adjoining room and hit a button underneath the desk. The alarms stopped. "Everyone stay put. The doors are secure," Matt told them. He ran to the windows, pulling down metal sheets attached to hinges that locked at the bottom. The others followed at each window, pulling down the metal protection sheets, blinding them from the outside world.

A rabid "dog" threw his massive paws on the window before they could pull down the metal sheet, smearing blood and dirt on the pane with claws sharp enough to leave deep grooves in the glass. The scratching gave a high-pitched scraping sound. Horns of pointed stubs on the top of his head submerged out of his ratty fur, face sunk in. Two red eyes glowed like embers in a fireplace. Sven closed the protective metal to block his view, his hands shaking as he hooked the latch.

"Devil dog," said Jesse, who was standing right next to Sven, sealing the adjacent window. "Holy shit."

"The MCS are on their way," said Matt. "They'll let us know when the coast is clear. We have weapons if necessary."

Matt led them to a hallway and unlocked the closet door tucked in so well it blended in, unveiling tranquilizer guns, knives, and shotguns.

"What about the women at the front desk?" asked Adam.

"They both went home when I was giving you the tour. You're the last customer of the day," explained Matt.

The mutant picked a nearby window, scratching behind the metal, making a squealing sound with its claws as it had a low growl, like an alligator nearing its prey. All the men grabbed the nearest weapon they could find. More scratching sounds echoed from other windows. The men stared at each other, looking for answers without speaking.

"Where's your security?" asked Sven with a growl not unlike the mutant.

"You're looking at it," said Matt, pointing at the objects in the closet. "The MCS are usually pretty fast getting here."

The scratching was louder and came in at more angles.

"You see why I wanted to get inside?" remarked Jesse in a snarky tone. "Well, I'm not just going to sit here." He picked up a shotgun and a knife, rushing toward the front door. Yanking on the handle, it wouldn't budge.

"It's best to wait for the MCS," urged Adam.

"What do you think you're doing?" asked Sven. "You're going to get us all killed."

Jesse stepped back from the door with a huff, joining the other men. They stood in a circle facing outwards, so if anything gave way, one of them would see it. Even with the lights on, covering the windows darkened the room and made it feel more closed in.

Sven took a deep breath, gasping for air. He then calmed himself, staring at the areas where the clawing and the growling traveled. The mutants were looking for access to enter. Sweat pooled in the palms of his hands and he almost dropped his gun. A rock formed at the base of his throat. They all stayed quiet, moving as little as possible.

Men and women screaming at each other came from outside, so muffled it was hard to decipher, but the MCS leaders were instructing others. Sven jumped as shots rang outside, one hitting the metal on the opposite side of the window.

"In the right-hand corner," Matt mentioned. A one foot square screen turned on. Divided into two different pictures, the right one displayed the far angle while the left one was a more in-depth view, more focused on the front door. "They're on motion sensors. I don't know why it took them so long to activate."

Sven stared at the screen, then around him, paying attention to his area in case something else went awry. The building seemed secure, but he saw what happened when things weren't always what they seemed.

Three mutants were visible on the screen, one of them being the "devil dog" that they saw earlier. The mutant had abandoned scratching the windows after being shot once, limping away as blood poured from his wounds.

A three-foot lizard-like creature had attached himself to the building with multiple legs that resembled a spider. Spikes jutted out of his leather-like gray skin, attaching him to everything. When he opened his mouth, there were no teeth, but a tongue that wrapped around an outside security camera and swallowed it whole.

The left side of the screen in the building went black.

The third mutant Sven stared at, wondering how he had gotten into the impure water supply. With the animals, it happened more often than not, but humans were a rarity. The man towered at eight feet tall with large hands and tiny fingers. Fish gills embedded on either side of his neck pulsed open and closed as if searching for water. The blood-filled eye sockets continued to bleed as he stumbled along with clown feet, easily a size twenty-four, bare and black.

"Oh, my God," Adam breathed. "How could he even be a threat? The poor man."

The lizard wrapped his tongue around the man's ankles, knocking him over, the man's head striking the ground. It kept striking the man's head against the cement until the skull cracked and brain matter flung everywhere. The MCS continued to shoot, unable to get too close for their own safety.

Five shots rang out.

Silence.

The devil dog lay bleeding against the building by the front door, a heap of fur matted with crimson red.

The lizard was in pieces with the continued shooting.

The man was unrecognizable compared to when they started watching. MCS men and women moved in closer to check the condition of the mutants, making them visible on the screen. For the safety of all, they disregarded the standard protocol of keeping the mutants alive.

The devil dog twitched twice and attacked one MCS, clawing and biting with no success. The man was tall and strong with preventative gear built strong enough to protect from an explosion of high magnitude, pulling out his gun and shooting the dog twice in the head.

Everyone in the circle stayed still after the noise subsided outside. Matt was the first to move, edging toward the entrance, holding a gun close to his side in defense. They all jumped when there was a pounding on the door. Sven jumped at the noise, giving himself a light cut on his arm from the knife he was grasping.

"It's okay to come out," the voice said from the other side of the door. "The perimeter is secure."

Matt hesitated.

"Is everyone in there okay?" the man from the other side of the door yelled.

Matt unlocked the door and eased it open. The MCS man that fought with the devil dog loomed over them, panting. There were scratches on his suit, but no holes or rips. Covered in blood that was not his own and dirt smudged on his face and in his hair, masking the true color.

"It's safe," he said, "And if everyone in here is good, we must return to home base before another call comes through. Our clean-up crew will be here shortly."

"Thank you," said Matt, and all the others chipped in with their thanks.

"Just doing my job. No thanks necessary," he said, turning quickly to walk away. After a glance to the left and right, Matt slammed the door shut. Leaning against it, Matt hung his head forward before looking up, as if he had forgotten the other men were there.

"You can take care of all the paperwork another day," said Matt. "We have our hands full here. I need to check on the entire facility. Perhaps on your first visit? You are more than welcome to visit your wife any time during business hours."

"Yes, that would be fine," Sven agreed, coughing into his hand. The rancid smell of the mutants outside seeped through the cracks in the building and when the door was open. "I've had enough excitement for one day. Going home to rest sounds just what I need." Sven thought of what had just happened and pulled back from the exit. "On second thought, are you sure that you don't need a hand checking the facility? We would all be happy to help."

"We have it handled," assured Matt.

"Let's go," said Jesse. "It's okay. We'll all watch out for each other. Did you want me to bring the jeep around?"

Sven shook his head.

They all walked out together, and Sven covered his nose with his hand, focusing on the straight shot to the jeep. As much as he tried, he couldn't avert his eyes to the scene, knowing he had to always be aware. Blood and brain matter smeared the side of the building. A slimy indentation of the reptile outlined on the wall, footprints in a trail where it had traveled. The dead dog lay on the top of the bushes while the pieces of the human mutant were everywhere, along with fragments of the lizard.

Jesse grasped onto Sven's arm and pulled him along to hasten him into the vehicle. Speeding up around a corner, his mini boxing gloves dangling from the rear-view mirror almost flew off.

"Jesse, slow the fuck down." Adam gripped the back of Jesse's seat. "Before you kill all of us. Let me drive."

"Language," reminded Jesse. "Think of Camille. I'm fine, and so is my driving." He eased up on the gas along with his grip on the wheel. "I'm just trying to get as far away from that place as I can."

"Here, fiddlesticks will not cut it."

"Just shut up!" Sven flung his arms around, nearly jumping out of his seat. He suddenly became still, surprising himself with his own reaction, before rubbing his forehead.

Adam leaned back and slumped in his seat, and Jesse stared forward, unable to look at either of them. "Now that's better." Jesse opened his mouth to say something, then paused and remained quiet, turning on music as the instrumental opening of the group "Smashing Boulders" played before the lead guitarist yelled through the radio.

Adam groaned, holding his hands to his ears.

"Sorry it's not Led Zeppelin, Grandpa," said Jesse, glancing at Adam.

Sven was thankful that Adam didn't say a word, but he was glad for the change of topic, not wishing to fight or have to defend himself any longer. The few miles home felt like an eternity.

Reaching home, they pulled into his garage via remote in Sven's pocket. After the door closed, Sven exited the jeep, moving at a snail's pace in total silence.

"Sven..." Adam said.

Sven looked back at him. His head hung low, taking a deep breath before exhaling.

"If you need anything, we are just a phone call away," Adam finished.

Sven entered the house and tried to slam the door behind him, but his fatigue resulted in a quiet close. Going straight to his room, he curled up in a quilt that Hannah had made. While lying down in bed, Sven couldn't take his eyes off of Hannah's empty hospital bed.

And he did not sleep.

—·—

# Chapter Four

S mog hung low in the air, thinner than the previous years, but Sven wished it was gone. An early morning rain drizzle created a mist and the scent of wet earth and pine sifted through the vents as he drove to the forest. Unable to continue struggling with sleep, he felt an urgent need to get out of the house. Remembering the travesty outside of the cryonics facility, he slipped the two most convenient weapons he had handy: a tranquilizer gun and a knife small enough to carry easily, sharp enough to cut through bone. He was glad he brought his warm jacket.

"Maybe I can find one or two of those tree frogs tonight," he muttered, returning to the origin of where they had found the secret ingredient for the serum. The rain intensified, making it harder to see, even with the defrosters and wiper blades. *Was that an excavator on the land?* A dump truck sat near the excavator, and he moved closer to see more construction vehicles that were digging ditches in the soil.

Scattered in the distance, he could see the MCS (mutant containment services). They are ready at a moment's notice after a 999 call to contain the mutants and take them to Juniper Ridge. They have a home base, take shifts, and have emergency vehicles. A burly powerhouse with protective clothing from bites, deep scratches, or puncture wounds surveyed the scene armed with a paralyzer gun that could freeze a mutant for a full ten minutes.

Hands choking the steering wheel, he sped up and almost ran into a parked Audi-glide. Slamming on his brakes, he stopped inches from it.

Sven climbed out of his BMW and wrapped his coat tighter around himself, glaring at the Audi-glide. A major transition when all vehicles went electric by law, it went one further step when they could fly as well. Then came the Audi-glide in 2072 that could be a boat along with everything else. Something that could be everything was a crazy thought to him. *Who in the hell could afford an Audi-glide that would be out here? Who could pay for MCS protection of this magnitude?* Two more MCS were openly visible around the perimeter, and he was sure there were more lurking in the shadows. Someone stood surveying the entire scene. A tall, thin stature in a yellow parka pointed and commanded what was to be done.

Sven stomped over to the figure, screaming at him. "Excuse me, what is going on here?"

"Charles Williams," the man said, keeping his eye on his crew and one on Sven. Holding out his hand, he said, "Pleasure to make your acquaintance." Given the weather and the early morning, all that Sven could see was the man wearing glasses perched on the end of his beaklike nose that he continued to push up.

"Sven." He shoved his hands in his pockets, not sure if he wanted to touch this stranger. They kept warmer, anyway. Charles Williams sounded familiar. Somewhere in the financial section of the newspaper, perhaps. The teleportation company! More than that, he was one of the wealthiest men alive. He was massive in pharmaceuticals and security, and who knows what else? He must have been the one that owned the Audi-glide. His shiny shoes and expensive parka looked out of place in the woods.

"What is going on out here?" repeated Sven. "This is private property."

"Yes, it is. I bought it." He spoke with a snap in his voice and finality. "I plan on expanding my company, and this is the perfect land to do so. So much space."

"You can't do that. No one can own the land out here. It's in the forbidden zone." The forbidden zone was the land where there were no safety measures from the mutants. No tall fences, cameras, or security. It was against the law to enter these areas for everyone's own safety.

"There is no 'forbidden zone' anymore, my dear friend. The world is different. Changing. It has become safer for everyone, and I plan on taking advantage of that. Besides, until I can add security to my building, I have the MCS to help for safety."

"You can't do that!" Sven's nostrils flared as he pointed to all the men that were working on the land. "This is all wrong. You can't do whatever you want." He stomped up to the excavator to reach the man sitting at the controls, but there was no way he could. Sven pounded on the side of the equipment enough times for the operator to shut it off and look down. Sven's hands were already beginning to ache from the pounding as he fought through the exhaustion.

"Stop that!" Charles stomped up to Sven. "Now, if you would please leave, or I will call the authorities."

"How far is this teleportation company going to reach?" asked Sven. He pictured the tree, the whole reason he had come out to check on it. While most of the trees in the world were sickly with dead branches, the tree that held the frogs had a rich brown to its bark, the leaves were green with an iridescent sheen, and a glow around the perimeter that is impervious of the present disasters. A dome-like massive structure of steel built around the tree for protection that resembled a fence with slots wide enough to allow sunlight, but small enough to enable most things to permeate through the barrier. A door with slots like the rest of the dome blended in on one side, with hinges and a latch so someone could enter to take the tree frogs for the serum. God forbid a mutant destroy it. The scientists named it the tree of life. The scientists and a handful of authorities only knew the location and how to get past the protection.

*More like the tree of secrets.*

"Just a few miles," he smirked. "It will work perfectly. Imagine all the advantages that it will have. It will change transportation as we know it. In emergency situations, imagine what will happen if help can get there instantly. It can save lives. It's not just for my benefit."

"How many miles are a few miles?" Sven asked again. *The tree is five miles away from here, and as long as he doesn't own that, or the surrounding areas, it will be fine.*

"Five miles, give or take," he said with a shoulder shrug. "Hey, I don't pay you to sit there. Get to work!" he yelled to the excavator operator.

The excavator turned back on and the operator manned the controls once more.

"You can't do this. It isn't right." *He doesn't know about the tree of life. Only Juniper Ridge and a handful of others know of the active ingredient source of the serum. Convince him.*

"An expansion of my company will better the world. Transportation will improve along with my profit. Everyone wins." Charles opened his arms, the rain dripping off his hair, ticking as it hit his coat.

Sven sniffled. The temperature was dropping, and he was getting drenched as the rain intensified. "It's not about profit."

Charles pulled back with a disgusted look.

"It can't be easy to work in this weather. You should just call it a day," argued Sven. *Call it a day until I figure something out because, obviously, I'm not getting anywhere.* The excavator moved slowly on the soft ground, but he continued to scoop up the ground into the back of the truck. "Do you really need all that land? I know of a lot of other places where the land is just as good. Maybe not as vast..."

"I don't think so. I like this land. Look, we have a lot of work to do, and it appears you are getting soaked to the bone. I bought the land legally, and it is mine. If you want to talk to the state about it, you go right ahead. They are the ones that sold it to me. You should get inside. You look like a drenched rat."

Sven dreamed of wiping the smirk off his face.

"It's not safe to be out here with the construction and don't forget, this is 'the forbidden zone'," mocked Charles. "Why do you think I hired the MCS?"

"Where's your hard hat?" *Not like there are any brains to salvage.*

"I'm just supervising, and well past the boundaries of the construction site. I could say the same to you."

"I didn't know I was going to be walking into a construction site."

"Fair enough." Charles looked up at the sky as thunder boomed. "Maybe we should resume this tomorrow." Lightning flashed moments later, brightening up the sky. "Yes, that would be best." Charles instructed the driver to call it a day, and the man climbed off the equipment. "Happy? What did you do? Control the weather?"

"Not me. Someone else must be telling you the same thing." Sven's snicker was too hard to contain.

Charles shook his head. "I am not doing anything illegal. Just building on my land. If you're smart, you will leave it alone."

"Is that a threat?"

"Just a piece of advice." He smiled at Sven, which aggravated him even more. "Now you can get off my property, or we are going to have a problem."

Growling extended beyond the trees, audible over the storm. Both men stopped and surveyed the scene. Sven grasped the knife attached to his belt in earnest and wished he had a weapon where he didn't have to get so close. Reaching onto his other side, he remembered the tranquilizer gun. Every member of the MCS was watching as well, weapons at the ready. In the distance, trees rustled as a creature emerged from them.

A lion's head with elk-like antlers and a cheetah body burst through the woods, massive and muscular. Three feet of a thin tail whipped haphazardly, its tip coming together in a point. Blue eyes bulged from its face that hypnotized Sven. He stared back at it.

The creature howled as two tranquilizer guns from MCS personnel on either side of it shot arrows that zipped through the air, but the mutant moved toward a man in full MCS gear, swiping at the man's chest and leaving scratches on his protective clothing, his torso unharmed.

He let out a ferocious growl, saliva dripping from his canines. The man lost his footing from the creature's attempt and fell on his back in the sticky mud, moving his right hand to retrieve the paralyzer gun from where it had fallen, but his arm wasn't moving.

Sven was several feet from the creature. Many others were closer that could intervene, so he stayed in wait in case the monster moved near. Sweat gathered on his brow and his breathing became erratic. His gaze never left the mutant.

Gunshots rang out from different angles, the mutant almost collapsing on the injured man before he pushed himself out of the way with his heavy boots. The air was a mixture of blood, nature, dirt, smog, and gunpowder. Blood poured out of the mutant's injuries as the MCS man that was almost crushed stood, his right arm hanging loosely at his side.

"Thank you," he said to his crew after wincing when he moved. "Thanks for not missing and shooting me, too."

They attended to the injured man first. Afterwards, they surrounded the creature and heaved him onto a huge cart-like device with hydraulics to lift him into the back of the MCS that emerged from the shadows.

With the threat gone, Sven glared at Charles.

"See?" said Charles, pointing to the scene. "That's why we have the MCS. It's perfectly safe." Charles tremored, fiddling with his glasses.

"Yes. So safe," Sven snarled back. Sven stomped back to his car. Mud flew from his shoes and he shivered from the cold. *The nerve of that guy. He doesn't own the world, and he certainly doesn't own me. He is going to get someone killed. If he destroys that tree, it will be harder to replace the serum that is declining, maybe even impossible and we will have more creatures on our hands than ever before. He won't even know what he is demolishing. Unless somehow he knows about the tree. If he doesn't, I'm certainly not going to be the one to tell him. Those tree frogs are our only hope, and there's something about that land.*

*The land doesn't like him.*

*I am losing my mind.* Sven made it back to the car, and wished there was a way he could check out the tree without Charles knowing, but Charles was watching his every move. He could feel the guy's eyes on him, making him shiver from more than the weather. There was something about him that was off, and he intended to find out what it was.

Turning up the heater in the car's cabin, it took a few minutes to warm up before he warmed his hands. Frowning at the mud that flaked on the floorboards and the water pooling on his seat, he peeled off his jacket and sighed. Once he was warm, he checked all of his mirrors, adjusted them, and put on his now dry jacket from the heated seats in the back. Treading the entire way around the car, he checked the tire pressure with his gauge, then returned to the comforts inside. Backing up, he took one more look at Charles before he left. "You're not going to win this one," he said. "I will be back."

# CHAPTER FIVE

That afternoon Sven mentally reviewed the remaining patients and felt relieved they were all on the same floor. "I just want to finish so I can go home. I'm so damn tired," he told himself as he left one of the patient's rooms.

Josh Freeman stopped him in the hall. "Sven, I'm glad I caught you. I don't have a lot of time, but if you have a few minutes, I would like to have a word with you."

His handshake was strong and deliberate, and his eyes were a dark blue with small irises. Sven followed him down the hall to an office that was well over the size of Sven's, speeding up his gait to keep up with the new lead. He flashed back to days going to the principal's office. His palms became sweaty, and he scolded himself. *This is your domain. No need to be fidgety.* Freeman looked behind him to make sure Sven was still there and opened his office door with his fingerprint. He wondered if Josh was going to be anything like his brother, Daniel, the founder of Juniper Ridge. Impressively neat, with books lined up on one wall, a desk took up most of the room, and a leather chair was behind the desk. No personal effects whatsoever. Maybe he just hasn't had the time. Nothing like his brother.

"I've read everyone's file at this facility," Freeman said, picking up a tablet and swiping through a couple of pages. Sven swore he saw his name in the corner. "Yours has impressed me. I know you are highly intelligent and academically gifted. Starting college at sixteen and being head of the class has given you a lot of time to research, study, and learn. I trust you will share any findings immediately with me on the progression of the usefulness of the serum and the setbacks."

"Of course. We are all a team here." Sven went to lean on his desk to regain his balance from the speed-walking, but kept hands off the desk after Freeman's glare.

Freeman's eyes narrowed, and after a lengthy pause, he nodded. "Right, a team. A team for which I am in charge." He tossed the tablet before tapping his index finger forcefully on his desk. "I am well aware of what happened here, and rest assured, nothing like that is going to happen. Ever."

Sven gulped, unsure if the man was offering reassurance or a threat. "Glad to hear that," he said.

"As long as I run this facility, we will follow the rules. We make rules for a reason, and we must not break them. Do I make myself clear?"

Sven remembered breaking the mutants out of the facility and hiding them in the woods, away from Jill's grasp. They should have done it a different way. Things wouldn't have gotten so out of hand, and they still would have been able to defeat Jill. Maybe Adam wouldn't have turned mutant. But then, would they have ever found the tree frogs?

"Do I?" Josh repeated himself, straightening his tie, bringing Sven back to the present.

"Yes, sir," said Sven. Just getting off probation for the stunt he did last year, he didn't wish to return to the courtroom.

"Good. I'm glad we understand each other. And if you want to do anything out of protocol, you must have my okay first. We want the world to be a better place, don't we, Mr. Olander?"

"That we can agree on."

"That's right." After a long pause, Sven stood and waited for him to say something else, but he just said, "You may go. I will be checking up on you periodically." He looked up at a simple clock hung on the wall. "I always see Jill around this time and check on her progress."

Sven flipped around, anxious to get out of the stale office and away from the new head of Juniper. As he put his hand on the doorknob, Freeman said, "And Mr. Olander. I am sorry to hear about your wife. I give my condolences."

Sven nodded once. "Thank you, sir," and shut the door behind him as he exited, leaning against the wall in the hallway. *No need for condolences. One day we will be reunited, and I don't mean in the afterlife. In the meantime, this is the time to show Josh Freeman what I'm capable of.*

"I am going to show you," he said out loud to no one but himself. "This world will be a better place."

When Sven flipped around, Adam interrupted his thoughts, hurrying up to him. "I am sorry about yesterday," Adam said, putting his hand on Sven's shoulder. "With no idea of your plans, you caught me off guard. You don't have to be here today. Everyone would understand."

"Do you understand my decision now that you've had time to think about it?" Sven rubbed his forehead to ease a pounding headache. Dizzy from exhaustion, Sven's back and arms ached, along with his heart and mind. He spent most of the night cleaning his car from top to bottom, making sure everything was working properly.

Adam bit his bottom lip, and a long pause followed. "I can't say that I agree with it."

"You don't have to. It is my decision, along with the decision to work. What am I going to do at home?" *At least here I can do some good and help my patients.* He straightened his shoulders, and they popped, pain running down his arms. He let out a wince.

"Relax?"

Sven glared at him. "I just have a few more patients. What about you?"

"Not many. I need to leave a little early today," said Adam. "I told Camille I would sit in on her karate class."

Sven welcomed the change of conversation. "I'm proud of you." And he meant it. There was a time that Adam would just work and nothing else.

"I better finish up."

Sven thought about his confrontation with Charles and grabbed Adam by the arm to slow him down. Adam stopped instantly, his brow narrowed in concern. "I need to talk to you about something." Sven thought of the teamwork that Adam, Jesse, and he had last year with Jill, and said, "Jesse needs to be here, too. Have you seen him?"

"Give me a second." Adam tapped his wristwatch, and Jesse's face appeared in seconds. "Jesse, where are you?"

"Finishing up with a patient." Sven heard a bird squawking in the background. "I'm just giving her the daily dose today. Do you need me for something? Everything okay?" Adam raised his eyebrows in Sven's direction.

"I need to talk to both of you. It's about the serum," said Sven.

Jesse snapped a rubber glove off. "I'm on my way." Sven could hear Jesse put the mutant back in her cage.

"Floor three," said Adam.

"We can talk about this as we finish up the patients," Sven suggested. "Adam, are you sure you have time with Camille's karate?"

"Since it is the serum, I'll call her and let her know. She'll understand."

Sven scrolled through his list of patients on his iPad until Jesse arrived.

Minutes later Jesse hurried up to them. "Geez, think we'll ever get teleportation devices in this place?"

"Don't even get me started," said Sven, thinking of Charles. "Modern devices aren't the answer to everything. Besides, walking a little is good for the cardiovascular."

Jesse held up his hands, palm up. "Sorry I brought it up. Now, what's going on with the serum?"

"We have to whisper." Sven's voice dropped in volume. "I still have a few patients to attend to before I leave. The last thing we need are rumors starting from security or from one of the other doctors."

"One thing I learned about these cameras lately is that's to our advantage," said Adam. "The pictures are okay, but the audio is crackly."

"Good point," said Sven, guiding the men to his first patient. The mumbled growling became audible when Jesse opened the door. The mutant would have been a bunny, but the eyes were facing the opposite way, and instead of bunny feet, it had claws much like a crab, sprinting across the cage in laps around the perimeter. It reminded Sven of when he used to watch NASCAR.

"Thick gloves," warned Sven. "Those feet aren't only fast, but sharp. I have the scratches to prove it." They made sure the door was closed before washing their hands and putting thick medical gloves on.

Sven went to open the cage. "Come on, Molly, we aren't going to hurt you." Molly slowed at Sven's voice, but kept moving. "Could one of you grab the spidomed in the drawer? I should have it ready with the serum." The spidomed looked like a metal spider, and could administer serum in seconds through the skin instead of using the sharp points in years past.

He opened the cage and went to grab Molly, but this time she was too fast for him and bolted for the door. "Get her!" he yelled, leaping forward and missing her as she began her laps around the room. "She'll run into something. The poor thing can't see where she's going, just where she's been!"

"I got her," said Jesse, leaning over and sweeping her up in one swift motion. He held her as Sven moved aside her gray fur so Adam could dispense the serum.

"It's okay, Molly," Adam cooed to her. "We are almost done and we'll leave you alone." Molly instantly relaxed as Sven stroked her fur.

"You have that voice," said Sven. "You can help me with Molly anytime. Thanks, both of you." Putting her back in the cage, he said, "She usually gets a little tired after her medicine." She curled up in a corner of her cage and fell asleep.

"Sorry, Sven, but I don't think talking about this and taking care of patients is going to work," said Jesse.

"I guess you're right. Let's get this done," said Sven.

A fingerprint scan later, they were in Sven's office. He had upgraded in size over the years that he had worked at Juniper Ridge. The large L-shaped desk had three monitors on one side where he could watch parts of the facility that changed every minute or two, the other a computer and photos of him and Hannah on his right side, the other pictures of loved ones on his left. His wastebasket was full of crumpled-up papers and candy wrappers. He dusted, vacuumed, and cleaned his monitors daily, allowing no one else in without his presence. A spot of dirt on the photos of his loved ones was unthinkable.

Sven leaned against his desk. "Someone has bought the land of the tree of life."

"What? Who?" asked Adam, standing back a step as he began tapping his fingers on the edge of Sven's desk.

"How? I didn't think anyone could do that? Isn't it already owned by the ridge? Besides, it's included in the forbidden zone." Jesse flew his hands up in the air as his eyes narrowed. "No one is supposed to know about its medicinal qualities but the ridge and a handful of other people."

"If news got out about it, there would be chaos on the tree's property," said Adam.

"It was owned by the State of Oregon," said Sven, covering Adam's hand to stop the tapping, "but if you have enough money, you can buy anything. I thought considering how important it is to everyone's future, that wouldn't be possible. Charles Williams is the owner. I guess he doesn't care about the forbidden zone. I don't think he even knows what's there. It must be a mistake."

"Well, he must know," said Adam. Rubbing his chin, he paused and his eyes grew wide. "He owns one of the biggest pharmaceutical companies in the country. He can't monopolize that serum. We need it. The serum we're making from the replicated DNA we don't even know is working. If it's not straight from the tree, we don't even know if it will work at all."

"How does he know about it?" said Sven, tightening his hands into fists. "I hope there's not a spy here feeding him information."

"Maybe he doesn't, but if he does, he won't get away with this." Jesse raised his voice. "Now that I am on board, this situation is going to end now. I took care of Jill, and I'll take care of him, too." Jesse pounded his right fist into his left palm.

"Now, Jesse, this is a different situation. This will take careful planning, and all of us. A lot more than just you, or any one person for that matter," said Sven, crossing his arms.

"You can't do it without me," Jesse said. "You know I'm right."

Adam held his hands up and moved them as he spoke, softening his voice like someone would do to calm down a child. "We need to find his angle," said Adam. "For now, he's not doing anything illegal."

"That we know of," said Sven. "I can't get too far into the details. I thought it would be beneficial to let you know as soon as possible so you could keep it in mind and mull over any ideas."

"At least we have the new underground lab that they've been building on. We're still setting everything up." Adam paused, glancing at Sven, then at Jesse. "Have you two even been down there yet?"

"Between the patients and home life..." started Sven.

"Considering what happened last time, the thought gives me the creeps," admitted Jesse. "A little," he amended, widening his stance and crossing his arms. Sven wondered if that was the real reason Jesse got back into boxing after the dangers of the previous year, but reasoned protection from the mutants would be the best reason.

"It will just take a minute, but I have to show you," said Adam, his eyes lighting up and a smile extending from ear to ear. Before Sven could argue, Adam motioned them with his hand and was traveling back down the hall with such energy it appeared he was skipping.

"You would think he was going to Disneyland," Sven grumbled, but he couldn't argue that he was curious.

"Never been there," remarked Jesse, following close on Adam's heels.

Sven gripped the railing as he walked. *Maybe someday they'll rebuild after fixing what the mutants had destroyed, or maybe they will make something better in its place.*

Sven remembered the world's slow transformation after the virus. The number of animals with strange deformities were escalating all in the same area: the river that bordered the north of the town that dumped into the Pacific Ocean. Then certain people were acting strangely, so they began testing the water and found the virus. By the time they could control the water and purity measures, animals and people were beginning to grow hostile, some even suicidal. MCS was created, fences were built, and people watched every move they made, going nowhere without a weapon. The building of Juniper Ridge began soon after: the cure was the mission.

After descending the elevator three floors, there was another hallway that ended with a set of stairs. The men were well ahead of Sven.

"Adam?" Sven called, continuing down the stairs. "Jesse?" The area differed from the rest of the building, which Juniper Ridge had renovated once they took over the entire property The renovations of the underground area were still underway, and they were working on it as a special place to keep the serum. It was more difficult to get to and less foot traffic than the present place, and although it would be easier to catch someone entering the area, they would need extra security on it.

"Right here." Adam was adjusting the thermostat on the refrigerator compartment that he had just installed. "This is going to be some area when it's done, but it takes so much fixing up."

The once dirt walls were now steel. Clear glass over the re-frigeration compartments took up one wall with white shelving. A low hum reverberated in the air along with a breeze from a central fan made of slats on the ceiling. The handles to get into the refrigerators had finger pads at their bases for fingerprint security.

"Glass? Is that secure?" asked Jesse.

"Go ahead," said Adam. "Give it your best shot. Try to break it."

"I will not try to break it when we're in the middle of building it. Are you insane?"

Sven and Jesse both jumped back as Adam grabbed a nearby hammer and instantly began pounding on the glass.

Sven leaned into the glass once he knew Adam finished and exclaimed, "Not even a dent! Amazing."

"No one is getting in here," said Adam.

"At least we have this," said Jesse. "A lot better than the security upstairs."

Sven picked up an electronic tablet, scrolling through the orders. Since the serum's active ingredient discovery a month ago, Juniper Ridge was working toward perfecting the DNA replication for the serum along with adding other ingredients to improve its effectiveness. In a collaborated effort to save mankind, hospitals and pharmaceutical companies permitted the delivery of limited amounts for further study. Sven skimmed the list, stopping on the third name, not surprised that Charles Williams had ordered the limit.

Sven walked around the perimeter of the new storage facility, everything shiny and new. Undamaged. "Just thinking of what used to be down here." Blinking once, he saw the muddy walls with mutant body parts buried within until they discovered some weren't body parts at all, but still attached and not dead yet. Jill broke the laws by hiding all the mutant parts from her killing underneath the main floor of the building. According to the laws, killing mutants is only allowed when someone is in physical danger and it is impossible to safely contain the mutant. The time of the serum discovery, Jill trapped Sven, Jesse, and Adam, leaving them to fight for their lives with no weapons until they could find their way out. He took a deep breath. At least the smell was gone.

"I don't know. Feels like justice to me." Adam leaned against the wall, wiping sweat from his brow. "Installed two of these units today after I saw my morning patients."

"Yes, patients. I still have three, and honestly, I'm exhausted." Sven looked at his watch, flashing at him as it was nearing five. Hating to admit it, his headache was intensifying and his eyelids felt like boulders.

"Who?" asked Adam. "I will see them."

"I'll take two," said Jesse.

"And check on Pamela in detox," said Sven.

Jesse let out a scowl. "I thought she was going to jail. They arrested her, right?"

"And it didn't get out of her system as quickly as they thought. You know how the rules work. Adam, I would rather you do it. She might be ready to take the restraints off." All human admits, addicts and mutants, were strapped down to their beds until they proved to be safe.

"I can do that," said Adam.

"Don't worry, we've got everything under control," said Jesse. "I wonder what kind of security Williams has at his house. Maybe I can look into that."

"With all that money, who knows? We'll talk about that later. Thank you both so much for helping me out. I will see you to-morrow." And Sven hurried up the stairs, this one time agreeing with Jesse.

This would be a great time to have a teleportation machine.

— · —

# Chapter Six

Reaching the top of the stairs, Sven spotted a door ajar and went to shut it. *Who would be so careless?* All doors were to be closed for the safety of the patients and the doctors. Sven narrowed his eyes. *Jill's room. Is Josh still visiting her?* He slowed his step and perked his ears so he could hear without looking too obvious.

"Uncle Josh, I don't want to," Jill whined from the other side of the door.

"You must. It's the best for you, and for everyone. It will improve your condition," said Josh from inside the room.

Sven thought of how she had brought the condition on herself. Jill was the daughter of the founder of Juniper Ridge, Daniel Freeman. Single parent to Jill, losing him after he died trying to help a mutant hit her hard enough she wanted all the mutants dead, thinking that this was the answer to the world's problems. Jill thought she could create humans out of DNA experimentation, unable to be touched by the virus. So convinced that this would work, she used herself as a project and altered her

DNA with serious repercussions, much like the mutants at the facility. She almost killed Adam when he changed, along with Jesse and Sven, for helping him.

Sven narrowed his eyes and almost had his ear to the door, peeking through the crack to see what he could. Josh was blocking some of his view, but Jill wasn't moving around in the bed as he heard before. She laid so still; she may have even fallen asleep.

Sven stepped back just in time for Josh to open the door with one fluid motion. "Jesus, Sven, I didn't know you were there. Are you okay? I didn't smack you with the door, did I?"

"Missed me," said Sven.

Josh's cheeks were red, his muscles tensed, and he ran his fingers through his curly black hair. Around Jill, he seemed a totally different person.

"How are you?" Sven asked.

"I'm fine. She's better. You know, I hear you talk with your friends, and she's not as horrible as you say. You don't think I'm listening, but I'm very observant, especially when someone is talking about my niece."

"We don't say anything that we know isn't the truth." The door to Jill's room was closed and secure. "What happened to you all those years, Josh? After her father died, where were you?"

"In a situation out of the area. I was trying to help where needed when the virus started spreading like wildfire, and I got stuck. People thought I was against the cure. They misunderstood what I was saying and imprisoned me, framing me for things that I didn't do. That I would never do." His hands balled into fists at his sides as he jutted out his chin. "What's your story, Sven? I couldn't be here, but why didn't you step up to the plate and do something? Daniel's death obviously crushed her, and she's never been mentally stable in the first place. You could have worked to help her instead of destroying her. I was under the impression you were a doctor that likes to help people."

*How dare he?* Sven seethed, taking a deep breath. Everything on Sven's face tightened: his eyes narrowed, his lips pressed together, and the skin on his forehead stretched so taut he could feel his pulse. Sven reached for Josh's arm to ring some sense into him, but Sven pulled his hand back at his side. He wondered if the cameras were off, if his reaction would be so tame. Or if he didn't look so much like his brother, Daniel, that was so close to Sven. Or if he wasn't in charge at the moment to put this place back together.

"Let me get this straight. I help people. You obviously know her better than I do and could have found a way to be here if you love her as much as you say you do. You got here now, right?"

"Yes, I'm here now." Josh stared at the floor, stumbling over his reply. His crossed arms slacked and hung limp at his sides, his forehead creased in thought. "I will tell you one thing. I know Jill is a prisoner and that she did wrong. I am trying not to have that happen again, trying to protect her AND everyone around her. I'm overseeing the process to fix what she broke. Does that make sense?"

Sven's head throbbed, and he yearned to go home and relax, but he had a job to do. "I need to check on her." He looked over her chart on the computer before doing his examination. "She's vastly improving," said Sven. After putting on a pair of gloves, he reached down to touch her fingers, identical to the hands she once had before they turned into claws. Eyes closed; she slept. He pulled back her left eyelid and the puss had completely drained, although the right eye socket had never recovered. It left a hole as if the puss had liquified the eyeball and surrounding tissue, and seeped out.

"Do you think she's a candidate for an artificial eye?" asked Josh.

"I think she'll do fine with one eye. At least she got her hands back. She's lucky there. The fact that she isn't a mutant in the sense that everyone else is here says something about the serum. It cures more than just the virus from the water. I need to get home. We'll discuss this later, okay?"

"Okay. I'll just stay a few more minutes." As Sven left after making notes on the computer in the hallway, he stuck his head in the door and reminded Josh to keep the door shut for safety, and then closed it behind him.

Sven took a deep breath, hoping he could get out the door to get some rest before someone else stopped him and needed his help. With blinders on, he headed to the front of the building and made it all the way out to the car.

# CHAPTER SEVEN

After a night of somewhat restful sleep and his morning patients all taken care of, color had returned to Sven's face and the jitters of fatigue had gone. Sven looked around before opening up his computer, even though he was in his own office. Free of clutter like Josh's, the difference was he had personal touches. Picking up a picture of Camille as a toddler, her big blue eyes looking at the camera with chocolate all over her face, he remembered when Hannah had them over for dinner and made her famous chocolate chip cookies. Camille wanted two, one for each hand, so she had split it in half, and the child was happy. He wondered how losing Hannah was going to affect Camille. Hannah wasn't only his.

He covered his head with his hands. *Such a fool I've been! I haven't even called the family. Calling them will make it true, but remember, it's only temporary. She's not gone forever, and you will bring her back someday.*

Nathan, his nephew, was the first person who came to mind. He lived in California, which wasn't too far away. Tapping his watch and speaking Nathan's name into it, a picture of Nathan popped up on the screen.

"Hey, Uncle Sven," he answered, out of breath. Nathan's face was red and hair sticky with sweat. "Give me a second." Nathan swigged some water and got back on the phone. Sven paused, taking a deep breath, and bit his bottom lip.

"I was just calling to tell you…" The words were escaping him, as if saying it out loud would make it true.

"Aunt Hannah? Oh, I'm so sorry. I will get up there as soon as possible. You don't have to go through this alone." Nathan's eyes glossed over with tears. "I love you."

"I love you, too."

"Just let me take care of a few things. I will be on my way. Unfortunately, the teleportation machine doesn't travel that far. It might be a couple of days."

"It's okay. Take your time. I want you to be safe."

"I promise." Nathan clicked off the phone.

Sven was glad that Nathan stayed in his best physical shape. At least he had a better chance against a mutant with the weapons that he used. The virus had spread over most of the world.

Turning back to his computer, he tried to process City Hall, and found public records that showed property paperwork of the area. He had to make sure that Charles had legal documentation of the property. Charles bought it all right, and he leaned in, reading the details. He owned twenty acres of the land, but there was something fishy about the details of the property line and where it ended. There were two conflicting documents. One had the property line ending before it hit the tree with the frogs, and the other went well past the tree and another acre. Which one was right and which was a faux?

The answer was obvious to Sven. Now he just had to prove it.

Sven opened up the second drawer of his desk, and the smell of chocolate filled the air. His goody drawer was full of candy bars, cookies, and small packages of chocolate-covered sunflower seeds. He popped a bite-size Hershey bar in his mouth, and let the candy melt on his tongue, the sweet dessert filling his mouth as it made its way down his throat. He knew chocolate had gotten expensive because the ingredients were rare, but they were his guilty splurge.

Stomach growling, he supposed it was time to get some lunch. Chocolate, as delicious as it is, wouldn't do for a meal.

Just one more thing. He peered in his computer and looked at the details, trying to find the changes that Charles made in the property line, anything to prove alteration, but that two different ones existed should have been proof enough. A man at City Hall made the second change named Michael Stratford. It was time to pay him a visit.

His stomach growled again. "Yes, I hear you. Lunch, then we will see who this Michael Stratford is."

Sven threw a meatloaf sandwich in the heat-fast bag he had in the passenger seat to cook as he drove to City Hall. At a stoplight, he unzipped the bag and took a bite, the bottom half wrapped in a cloth reusable napkin. Moaning as the combination of spicy herbs and the smokey flavor of the bacon hit his taste buds, he rolled his eyes and the car behind him honked.

The light had turned green.

"Okay, okay," he said with a mouthful and put his lunch down. He knew he would have plenty of time to eat when he got to City Hall. The lines to get into the building were long, with all the mutant security measures. Five blocks down, he pulled into the driveway and felt fortunate he picked a good day with only four cars in front of him. He pulled out his lunch and finished every bite, being careful not to make a mess. He wiped everything down with moist towelettes, including his fingers.

Reaching the front of the line, the cameras blinked and the motion detectors were on. His car detected nothing outside, so he drove into an enclosed parking garage. Within were the doors to the City Hall.

Upon entering, everyone put their fingerprint on a reader for record keeping. Then another door opened to an information clerk. The man was an older gentleman; Sven guessed he had been working there a long time. His eyes scanned the entire room in a fluid, constant motion. "Good afternoon, Sir. Where can I direct you?"

"Michael Stratford, please."

"Take the elevator to the third floor and it's to the right or the teleportation machine." He pointed to an elevator across the hall with the archway of the machine next to it.

After Sven hit the "3" button of the elevator, he stepped back to allow four women to exit, all in business attire, a variety of ages. Clinching and releasing his hands into fists, three floors took seconds until he reached Mr. Stratford's door, his name in gold letters with the title "Land Manager" underneath. He lifted his fist to knock, but the door flew open by a man in a gray business suit, blue tie, and gold cufflinks.

"Can I help you?"

Sven reached out his hand to shake and noted Michael's firm handshake. "I'm Sven Olander and I have some quick questions about a property dispute. If you could clarify this with me, I would appreciate it. I only need a minute of your time."

"I could spare a few minutes. I have a meeting soon, so let's get started." Michael cleared his throat, opening the door wide for Sven to enter. "Doctor Olander, what can I do for you?"

Sven paused, then he realized the man's knowledge of his identity shouldn't surprise him.

"I am very active in the community," Michael clarified. "I know who you are and the very impressive work you are doing. What's on your mind? You said this was something about a land dispute." Michael continued to stand, eyeing the door while waiting for Sven to finish.

"Yes," he said, knowing this man must know about the tree of life, since a part of his job was to protect it. "The tree that has the source of the serum is my concern. Someone brought to my attention that someone may have purchased it."

Michael's face pulled back and his eyes widened. "I can assure you; this isn't true. We are to protect the tree at all costs. It's the future of our survival." Michael jumped back at his desk and fired up the computer in minutes, speaking to his watch phone. "Yes, this is Michael Stratford. I am going to be late. An emergency has come up." The person on the other end of the line asked if he needed to reschedule, and he convinced them he would be there shortly, but to hold his spot. Sven sat in the chair on the other side of the desk, watching him hit keys on his computer. Michael covered his mouth with his hand, leaning into the screen. Shaking his head, he said, "This can't be right." Sven waited for more, tilting his head to get a glimpse of the computer screen. "These land boundaries have been altered. Charles Williams owns the land adjacent to the tree, but the property line was an acre away from it." He punched in a few more keys and shut the computer down.

"Thank you," Michael said, standing and reaching out to shake Sven's hand. "We will visit the property to be assured that Charles Williams understands where his property lines are. How did you know about this?"

Sven paused. *I don't want to give myself away. Charles can't know I came here.* "I went for a drive and saw the construction in the area of the tree and wanted to make sure it was safe."

"We will make sure that a representative goes to the land and talks to the owner, so there is no confusion."

Sven's forehead glistened with sweat. He stammered, "They won't mention my name, now, will they? I'm coming in anonymously."

"Oh, don't worry, we will get this all taken care of. If you will excuse me, I am late for a very important appointment."

Sven exited the way he came. Traffic was maddening, which only added to his frustration. He wondered if Charles would find out he was the one that informed the city of his construction and what his next move was. Listening to his MCS scanner, he heard there was an incident in town with a mutant bobcat, and Sven knew that they would soon have another admit.

A black Range Rover with the front smashed in blocked the intersection. A woman slouched forward behind the wheel, unconscious. He could see the top of a little boy's head, the blonde locks reflecting off the sunlight.

Instantly transported to forty-five years ago, he remembered when the semi-truck turned in front of him, too close to have time to stop. The screeching of the tires on the wet pavement played in his mind like it was yesterday. The crash jarred Sven's body enough to knock the wind out of him. Airbags exploded, catching him in the face and impeding his view. His first thought was of the child in the back seat and if he was okay. The boy moved his hand a fraction of an inch before coming completely still. "Lucas?" Sven rasped, reaching out for him, pain pulling his shoulder. That was the last time Lucas moved.

The yelling and the sirens all around him broke him out of his trance and returned him to the present time. He surveyed the scene to see if he could be of any assistance.

In the distance, he could see the MCS and their jeeps. A burly powerhouse had a hold of an animal with a bobcat coat of fur, a wolf's head with a horse's tail that they were placing in the vehicle, surely frozen from the paralyzer gun.

A teenage girl held the side of her head and was crying as blood gushed over and through her fingers. A team of paramedics rushed out of an ambulance. One went to the girl to help her put pressure on the wound while another was prepping the spidomed. Sven found a place to pull over.

Looking everywhere around him to make sure that no other mutants were about ready to rush him, he went directly to the paramedics. "I'm a doctor. Can I help?"

"Absolutely. We could use all the help that we can get," the woman said, who was prepping the spidomed. She pointed to the carnage on the other side of the ambulance, where they gave him gloves and the tools he needed, a box of supplies: bandages, medicines, and tape. He tested vitals, held a man's hand as he cauterized a wound on his left leg. Sven inwardly grimaced at the mangled leg, hoping with everything that they had learned over the years, they could somehow save it. With new prosthetics, no one would know the difference, just the person, because the feeling would be strange. They could almost do it with a donation, but hadn't mastered that yet.

*Science has come so far. Thank God that I was going this way. I can help. I need to help.*

"Is he gone?" The injured one looked frantically around him, tensing up, and Sven was sure it intensified the pain as he did so.

"They have him. The MCS," said Sven. "He's gone. You're safe." Sven peered around. Just because the one mutant was captive doesn't mean that there weren't more in the vicinity. "I don't see anything." Sven spotted a man hunched over his steering wheel in a nearby car. "Just hold tight. I'll be back."

"I'm okay."

Sven rushed to the car and yanked open the door, trying to catch his breath. The other door was open. It appeared the mutant had gotten in from the other side and eaten a side of the moaning man's stomach, intestines, and anything else underneath the rib cage on the right side. *Oh, God. He's alive. I can't believe he's conscious.* "I just want to die," the man said. "It hurts so bad." Sven ripped the seat cover off and used it to put pressure on the wound, even though he knew he was just prolonging the inevitable.

"I'm here," said Sven, soothing him and speaking between breaths. "What's your name?"

"Brandon," he sputtered.

"Everything is going to be okay, Brandon."

Brandon reached over to Sven and held a grip on his hand so tight that Sven couldn't believe the strength. "Stay," Brandon breathed. Sven wasn't going anywhere, and let this stranger that was dying right in front of him hold his hand. *Oh, God, how was he going to deal with all this dying?* "Tell Mary I love her," he said, "and I'm sorry." The man's grip slackened, and he hunched over the wheel, the car horn going off.

"I promise," said Sven.

A few people glanced his way as the horn blared, but everyone was busy cleaning up the wreckage and securing the perimeter so no new mutants could attack while they administered medical care.

Sven leaned back to the man that looked like he was in his early thirties, close to Adam's age. Everyone has been trying to talk him into retiring, but how could he even think of that when there was still so much more to do?

Sven stumbled out of the car, covered in blood from trying to stop the wound from gushing, and noticed they were putting the young man he was helping earlier in the back of the ambulance.

"Thank you for your help." One paramedic came up to Sven. She had a tattoo on her right shoulder of a lion and her cubs. A perfect lion before the change.

"Glad I came along," he said.

"I am sure we have this under control. Rumor has it they lowered security on the north end of town because of the new cure." She made quotation marks in the air with her fingers when she said new cure. "That was an idiotic idea." Her brow narrowed, and she cocked her head. "You look familiar." She waved her finger at him. "Were you..."

He finished the line for her. "Yes, I was one of the scientists that discovered that entire operation with the DNA experiments. Just one scientist, mind you. We all worked together to get it done, and now things are going to be much better."

"I hope we can get there." They both took time to look around. Blood soaked the street. Cars were smashed from running into each other to get away. Shattered windows littered the pavement and there was a smell that lingered in the air of coppery blood, sweat, and something that he couldn't put his finger on.

"So do I." Sven sighed, rubbing his hands on his pants, leaving a smear of blood. "Well, I should go home and clean up. I was on my way somewhere, but I'm certainly not going to show up like this."

"Thanks again..."

"Sven." He shook her hand.

"Alicia." She gave him a weary smile. "Don't take this the wrong way, but I hope we don't cross paths again."

He smiled and walked away.

—·—

# Chapter Eight

After his excitement with the wreckage, Sven went home to clean up. His muscles ached as he moved through the house, shaking his head at the dirty dishes in the sink where he first went to wash his hands.

He scrubbed, taking his time, watching the dirt and blood change the color of the water to a rusty brown before it eventually came clear. Gripping the edge of the sink, he leaned forward. He could hear Hannah's voice. *Don't worry about the mess. You saved lives today. You deserve a rest.* She always thought he was working too hard. And as always, she was right about the rest. *I'm so tired.*

Heading upstairs to the shower, he wished now they had bought a one-level home. The hot water felt fabulous for his sore muscles and the terrible memories of the day seemed to run down the drain along with the grimy filth.

He thought of Hannah. Shortly after they were married, an awful storm was coming where they had lost all their electricity. Windows boarded up so the harsh winds wouldn't blow tree branches or other debris against them and break. They had lit every candle in the house around their living room, leaving a mix of scents in the air of cinnamon, hemlock, and strawberry. The glow from counters and tables randomly gave it a romantic, yet seance-like atmosphere. Curled up on the end of the couch, Hannah told stories about growing up in the forest and living in the trees as a squirrel. Sven told her she should write children's books, and she laughed at him.

Dressed and clean, he headed downstairs, stopping for just a second to sit on the end of the couch and catch his breath. Knots formed in his stomach as he thought of his promise to Brandon. He tapped the seat next to him as if summoning Hannah with a touch. "I miss you," he said, before leaning forward and his eyes closed.

After awakening minutes later, he rushed back to work, but first he needed to stop by Mary's. With a quick call to Alicia at the local paramedic's station, he explained the situation and she gave him the address, although it was against protocol, and wished him luck. She even offered to join him, knowing how difficult it would be. He convinced her he would be fine.

Mozart filled his car on the way to the address that she gave him. Deep breaths. He yearned for one calm day, but didn't see one anytime soon. Knowing the authorities wouldn't have made their way to her house yet because they had their hands full with the travesty, he pulled on to a driveway in front of a house much like his own. Motion sensors beeped for two minutes before turning off. A screen turned on near the entrance of the garage on the driver's side and a young woman's face flashed on the screen.

Turning off his music, she asked who he was.

"I need to speak to you about Brandon."

With a curt nod, the garage door opened. Waiting for it to shut behind him, he reached the door to see Mary in a sweatshirt and jeans, her arms crossed in front of her. Her wide stance blocked the entrance.

"Where's Brandon? He was supposed to be home from work by now. I was about ready to start making phone calls." Her voice shook as she peered behind him into the car.

"He asked me to come. There was an accident." Sven stepped slowly up to her as her face fell, her mouth dropped open, and her nose scrunched up.

"No," she said, shaking her head. "It wasn't the..." Sven gave her time. "I just saw on the news and somehow I knew."

"Yes," Sven said, his voice dropping as tears fell from her eyes. "I'm very sorry. He wanted me to tell you that he loved you. I was there with him."

Covering her face in her hands, her tears turned to sobs until she was out of breath. Sven moved toward her, but she held up her hand. "Just give me a minute." Bloodshot eyes looked up at him. "Did he suffer? What happened to him?"

"Brandon sustained injuries from the mutant attack and fought for his life, but the severity of his injuries was just too much. No, he didn't suffer," he lied.

"Good," she said. "That he wasn't hurting."

"He wanted me to tell you that he loves you and that he is sorry." Sven didn't know what to do with his hands, feeling like useless limbs hanging from his sides, and shoved them in his pockets.

"And thank you for telling me, for being there for him. If you will excuse me, please." She turned to retreat into the house when Sven reached out to her. But what would he say? The door behind her slammed shut and a moment later, the garage door opened after he was safely back in the car.

And now, it was time for patients' healing to get their serum. They had to keep fighting and cure the mutants, or he would be making more visits he didn't want to make. After he made it to work he went down to the lab to gather the necessary doses.

With the lights dimmed, Sven almost didn't notice the figure in the corner. *So much for security.* "What do you think you're doing?" he said before flipping on the light.

In the corner, Adam was bent over, arranging an aquarium. "Sorry," he said, glancing behind him. "I didn't mean to scare you, Sven. It's just me."

"I can see that." Sven blushed.

"I'm just finding a proper place for the tadpoles. We have to keep them safe, too, right? More frogs, more serum, less mutants..."

"Since they aren't serum yet, at least they would be harder to steal." Sven watched the tadpoles swim in the tank. "A treasure you are," he spoke to the swimmers. "You may be the answer to the biggest problem of the world." Sven remembered when he was a boy and they used to play with tadpoles and catch them by the river. At seven years old, he didn't know how important they would be in the future. They were just tadpoles. "You're coming up with some good ideas, Adam. Keep it up."

"I will try, believe me."

"Meanwhile, we will see what any of these other facilities come up with. I just need to pick up some serum for the patients, and I will be on my way." He perused the list of patients and their dosages on his printout before using his fingerprint to open the refrigerated compartment. Open, the green serum reflected off the interior lights of the fridge. Each row of vials was different amounts, which he placed in a nearby empty caddy for transportation of medicines. He thought of all the good that it was doing for the mutant patients, and if it could be good for anything else as well.

*I wonder what it could do for Hannah? If the dose changed, ingredients altered perhaps...*

"Just remember to close that tight when you leave," said Adam. "We don't need anyone getting in there that isn't supposed to be."

"Don't worry, I will."

"See you upstairs." Adam took another look at his handiwork, smiling at the aquarium before leaving, Sven right behind him.

On the way up, he ran into Josh.

"Are you busy?" asked Sven.

"Why?"

"I need to finish with the serum injections by the end of the day for the entire floor, and I haven't even started."

Josh bit his bottom lip. "Well, I haven't been here very long. Maybe we can do it together? I can document and you can inject. It still will go faster that way."

Stopping at the first room, Sven looked through the room's binder to check the notes and dosage. Squeaking came out of the room so softly someone would have to listen to hear it. They entered, and there was a tiny kitten in a cage, an eye missing, an extra foot extending from one leg. One side of the mutant was gray fur, the other scales.

"It's so tiny," said Josh, leaning down to get close to the kitten.

"This is Ginger. You should have seen her before we started using the serum. The sores healed. She was so violent." Sven took Ginger out of the cage and petted her. "How are you this morning?" The kitten purred.

Sven sat her on a nearby counter, where she was relishing all the attention. "Want to hold her while I inject the serum? You better put these gloves on first. She's not used to you." Sven handed him a pair of thick leather gloves.

"Thanks, but I don't need the gloves." Josh at first held her at arm's length like she was a bomb until she squirmed. He pulled his head back while shifting his gaze to Sven.

Sven had to fight from laughing.

"How's this?" Josh asked.

"Maybe a little closer to you," Sven said, "and she won't squirm as much."

A forked tongue jetted out of her mouth, and Josh nearly dropped her. "You could have warned me."

Sven noticed at least two scratches where trickles of blood were forming. "Are you sure you don't want gloves?"

"Maybe that's not such a bad idea." Sven held her while he put on gloves and grasped the mutant again. "Will you hurry already?"

"Just 4cc is all we need. She's a little thing. She doesn't need much. Sorry," Sven said to Ginger, and spoke sweetly to the cat to calm her down.

"Not very friendly," Josh said.

"I don't think you would be friendly either if you were stuck in here with medical problems. Don't worry, she'll grow on you.

You should have seen what she did to me when she first got here, but now she's feeling so much better." While Josh held her down, Sven laid the spidomed against her scaly side, pressed, and was done. "Think you could handle the paperwork?"

"Of course," said Josh, passing Ginger back to Sven after she cried and hissed in Josh's grasp.

"Are you feeling much better?" Sven asked Ginger, examining her. He lifted up her fur, and she looked healthy underneath. "You're looking much better."

He turned his attention toward Josh. "Did you want to put her back in the cage?"

Josh's eyes grew wide. "I think I will leave that to you."

Josh opened the cage door wide and Sven placed her inside, closing the door in one fluid motion. The smell of urine filled the room. "Looks like someone is going to have to clean this room up soon." Sven picked up the book again from the outside of the room, showing Josh where to put in the updates from the cat, always eyeing the cart with the serum.

They continued down the hall until they got to the end, Josh doing paperwork. Sven pulled out his keys, opening the closet at the end of the hall, shoving the cart in it, locking it with the key and combination.

"What are you doing? Don't you need that for the next patient?" asked Josh.

"Not this patient." Sven picked up the binder, thinner than the others, a clear plastic envelope sealed tight, sandwiched in the middle that contained the vial that she had in her pocket when admitted: the contents an off-yellow hue, black corked top and a red line down the side. "Jamie Clark. She's a serum addict. They send them here because we know the most about the serum since we created it. We aren't only treating her, but she's being studied." *What batch did she get her serum from with so many pharmaceutical companies experimenting? Maybe that was a part of the problem, but then again, these are the people that are making the shortage. They are destroying themselves at the same time. A perfectly normal body. Maybe not totally healthy, but normal. But I have to be professional. I'm here to help people and animals. I am a doctor.*

They entered the room and found Jamie with wrist and ankle restraints. She had entered a deep sleep, her eyes rapidly moving as she snored. The bed smelled of sweat. Sven saw demons in his mind. Ten feet tall with horns and many eyes that could see him from any angle. The bloodshot eyes had no lids, but were always watching.

Josh jumped back.

"Yeah, I almost forgot to warn you," said Sven. "Too much of a good thing, that serum and the addicts can implant almost anything in your head. Sometimes they don't mean to. A lot of them don't even realize they are doing it. Right now, we are probably watching her nightmare." Jamie pulled against the restraints and whimpered. "We need better education for these young people. It's more than just getting a high. It's dangerous to the body and the mind. We must help her before she goes insane. How much of this could you take?"

"I would rather not find out." Sven opened the drawer of a cart in the corner with his fingerprint and sedated the girl. "You think you can manage a temperature while I take her blood pressure?"

"Sure." Josh pressed the thermometer against her forehead. As the sedatives took effect, the picture of the demon faded from Sven's mind until it was only a memory.

"So, what can we do for them?" asked Josh.

"That's what we are trying to figure out. Keeping them off the stuff, sedated so they can live through the withdrawals and see what happens. Try to preserve their body and mind as much as we can. Sometimes they can't take it. I've seen people die from these overdoses, and I've seen them go mad."

"What happens to the mentally ill ones?"

"Some are in padded rooms and we watch them closely. We've had two suicides. You're on the way to cure one thing, but it causes another problem. As long as we can control it, it can be a very good thing. It seems to be working. That cat came to us barely able to breathe, covered in scales of her whole body. She had numerous open sores and spots on her lungs. We've almost healed her."

Her lungs. He thought of Hannah, and his chest tightened again. Sven stared into space.

"Are you okay, Sven?"

"Fine. I think that's enough for today. We have everyone taken care of. I'll come check on Jamie later." Sven looked back at her, now sleeping soundly. Even the snoring had lowered to a slight roar.

Locking the door behind him, Sven grabbed the unused serum to return it to the lab. Even knowing it had been a short time since he was there, he did an inventory to make sure everything was in place.

Gazing at the large vial in the shadows through the closed glass door, he took a deep breath and walked away.

# CHAPTER NINE

The boardroom was spacious, with a large table in the middle and twelve plush seats lining the edges. Men and women dressed in business attire filed in, speaking amongst themselves at a low rumble. Some held notebooks, others electronic devices to keep notes, such as electro pads that resembled tablets. Most of the light came from the large paned windows on either side of the room, the overhead light turned off.

Charles entered the room and, instantaneously, people rushed to their seats and the talking ceased. Devices turned on in preparation to record the meeting. Charles placed a wooden box six inches square in front of him.

"I would like to thank you all for coming today. Everyone here in this room is the best in the field. You are all top pharmaceutical scientists and I expect nothing but the best from every one of you." Charles looked around the table, noting the group of twelve. He lifted an electronic notepad, hitting a button and a contract showed on the wall. "You are all to sign this document if you want to work on this project. Everything we find and talk about is confidential and only used by myself and this company. If you so much as think of betraying my trust, I will sue you like you've never seen. You will lose everything you own and you and your family will live out on the streets." He raised an eyebrow. "We all know how safe that is, don't we?"

An older woman's eyes grew wide, and she straightened up in her chair. Others fidgeted. Many turned their attention to the contract that simply stated everything that they created, discovered, and shared with the group would stay with the group.

"So, what is the project?" asked someone, breaking the silence.

"To learn that, you will need to sign. Anyone who works on this will receive a one million dollar bonus upon its completion."

More mutterings amongst themselves.

"So we don't even know what it is before we commit? What if it isn't a success?" asked another.

"No, you won't know until you sign, and it WILL be a success. Failure is not an option. Control is key, and this is how we take control." Charles lifted the box.

A young man narrowed his eyes and pointed at the box, hesitating before speaking. "So, what's in the box?"

"The essence of the project that you will undertake." Charles, after putting the box back down, sat in the chair at the end, resting his elbows on the table, tapping the end of his fingers together. "I will let you look over the contract and decide. Ten minutes." Charles slid the electronic pad across the table. "If you wish to join this endeavor with me, sign here, or leave without repercussions."

He watched the faces of the scientists before him, some of the most brilliant people in the world. Patrick stood first, took a deep breath, and signed his name. Charles nodded in approval. He had been working for the company since Patrick started his career as a pharmaceutical scientist and in the last fifteen years had grown vastly in both knowledge and experience. Patrick would love the challenge.

After he signed, more stood forward to sign, with three walking out. The ten minutes was up. After nine signatures, he was aware that everyone had been accounted for. Opening the wooden box, he lifted a container of vials full of the anti-mutant serum.

"We are strengthening this," he proclaimed, "strong enough so we can bring people back from the dead."

# CHAPTER TEN

Flipping on his television after a long day at the facility, Sven reclined in his easy chair with a root beer and the news came on. A news anchor stood in front of the local college with a grim expression.

"I am sorry to report today that three mutants made their way through the fences near the Arts Department of Panacea Community College this afternoon." Sven put down his soda and leaned forward, turning it up. "Twenty-five students and two facility members lost their lives today." Pictures of victims flashed on the screen, one at a time, their names on the bottom, along with their ages. Most were between the ages of eighteen and twenty-two, smiling, excited about the futures that were ripped from them. "One of the worst I've seen in years," Sven said to himself. He remembered what the paramedic told him about the security slacking off, and he was sure it was the same at the school. *Something had to be done or this will just continue. More serum in place and we can't keep our guard down!*

He turned off the TV, not being able to watch for another second. His mind filled with mutants and dead bodies covering the campus. He squeezed his eyes shut to block it out. *I can't keep watching from the sidelines.*

In his home office, he researched. Looking up the size of the property that Charles had, the price he paid, what he needed it for, he compared. "Charles is a businessman," he mumbled, "so I have to think the same." He shook as he thought of speaking with Charles, and a part of him thought he didn't have a shot, but he knew he had to try. He worked well into the night and afterwards tried to get some sleep. Morning came quickly.

Deep breaths. Deep breaths. "So, this is a bad idea," said Sven, talking to the empty seat in his BMW. Sven had showered and dressed in his best suit. "There are plenty of other places that you can build your company, and for so much cheaper. Profit is the goal, right?" Sven turned a corner, heading to the open road of the highway. "I hope he buys this. I didn't give myself a lot of time to prepare, but no way am I putting this off." Oh, God, I don't want to lose my nerve. The homes lined up taller and thinner every year with the growing population that once had fences surrounding them for protection had taken them down and rebuilt. Polycarbonate windows were no longer the thing of the past. Everyone had them with the lowered prices for low-income families. Nothing could penetrate these windows. Well, almost nothing, and they sure worked better than the previous bars.

Sven turned on the radio, speaking into it as it started the classical music that he was listening to on the drive before. It soothed him after a busy day at work, and any other stressful situation. He was sure this qualified.

He never played it with other people in the car. His music was private and for his ears only.

Reaching Charles' house, he pulled into the first driveway closest to the door, hoping it was the right one. A door closed behind him. Motion sensors scanned the area by infrared red lights, and Sven patiently waited. He had seen this before. The mutants were not as frequent, but the threat was returning.

He had tried to get out of his car when the coast was clear, but it was like there was a force field and he couldn't open the door. He heard a voice, "all clear", and he opened his door with ease, almost too much of an ease as the door flew open and slammed back to shut again. Sven stopped it with his foot.

Ringing the doorbell, he waited until a picture of whom he assumed was Charles' butler appeared on the screen next to the door.

"Can I help you?" the older gentleman asked. "Who are you and does Mr. Williams know of your visit?"

"Dr. Sven Olander. If you could let him know I would like just a moment of his time, I would appreciate it." Sven forced a smile, hoping his tension wasn't clear.

"Doctor?" asked the man. "Sven Olander." He squinted his eyes, trying to remember who he was.

"Yes, I'm one of the doctors from Juniper Ridge."

His eyes widened, and he smiled. "Of course. One moment, please."

Sven tried not to fidget, but he didn't know what to do with his hands or feet while he was waiting. *Please work.*

"Why don't you come in?" The door clicked, and Sven entered his house. He wasn't sure where the greeter had gone, but he was nowhere to be seen.

The entranceway was flawless, the marble white tiles swirled with blue reminded him of the ocean. A huge vase of purple roses, fake yet so realistic it was hard to tell, decorated a wooden table of dark oak. Lights hung from the ceiling in the shape of teardrops, which added to the whole ocean theme. Loud barking disturbed the quiet, and a golden retriever greeted Sven.

"Get back here," said Charles, following the dog. The golden retriever stopped, looked behind him, then looked up at Sven. If the dog could talk, he was sure the golden would say, "Save me, kind stranger."

"I'm sorry about Max," Charles said. "He was on the run after eating up my brand new shoes."

He stroked the dog on the head, calming him. "Oh, never mind, Max. Don't forget your manners."

Max trotted up to Sven and put his paw out for Sven to shake.

"It's a beautiful home," said Sven, although he was thinking of a fortress.

"Thank you. It's been in our family for as long as I can remember." Charles cleared his throat. "Mr. Olander, what can I do for you?".

*He's being too nice. We are both being too nice. Be careful.*

"First of all, I wanted to apologize for my rash behavior the other day. You are right. You bought the land fairly, and there's no disputing that."

Charles nodded. "Yes, you have done your homework, I see. Well, I am glad that we have agreed on something, Mr. Olander."

"Dr. Olander, if you may."

"Of course, *doctor.* I'm sorry." *I can't believe he is so affectionate with the dog. So he is human, after all.* "Did you come all this way for an apology, or is there something else I can do for you?" Charles didn't move, and Max sat directly to the right of his owner.

"I have a business proposition for you."

"I didn't realize that you were smart in the economic world, as well as the medicinal," said Charles. "I am very impressed. Dr. Olander," he said, emphasizing the word doctor. "Why don't we go into my office? If I would have known you were coming to see me, I would have been more prepared. One moment while I let Max out in the yard."

Sven followed him, but Charles stopped him. "Stay. That wasn't an invitation. I will be back. Don't touch anything."

Before departing, Charles obviously looked at all his cameras as if to tell Sven, I will be watching you.

"Stay," Sven muttered as Charles disappeared from sight. "I think he's nicer to his dog." It gave him a chance to look around. The cameras were Williams, the latest design. He had to try his own merchandise in his home. The man made a mint off of these things. Between the security, pharmaceutical company, and teleportation devices, the man was richer than God.

He did appreciate the cleanliness, although he was sure Charles didn't do it himself, being such a busy man. In the far corner of the room was a crystal-like archway huge in stature, with a keypad on the right side of it that almost blended in. Charles appeared seconds later, walking through the archway.

Fast. Of course he was. The teleportation machine.

"Impressed?" said Charles. "I could give you a deal on this one. It can go farther than any other one on the market, although I just use it locally. I don't have Max go through it though. It bothers him too much, and he always throws up on the carpet afterwards."

What carpet? Sven thought, but kept his mouth shut. He couldn't imagine Charles having anything actually comfortable, or anything that would be too hard to clean.

"No thanks," said Sven.

"You must have things to do," said Charles. "We better get this business meeting going." Charles waved Sven to follow him as they headed down a hall and stopped at the second door on the right.

Decorated with trinkets from all around the world, Incan masks hung on the walls and posters of show tunes from Broadway. A statue of the Venus de Milo about three inches tall was on a ledge with a gold Eiffel Tower covered with flecks of stone. A lighted corner display case with glass doors caught his eye. The statues and knickknacks nestled a trophy for track and field, the light gleaming off the runner's head. Reaching down to get a better look, he noticed a framed picture of a girl that looked around twelve years old, bowing from what looked like a school play, full of a toothy grin and squinted eyes. A bracelet hung from one side of the Eiffel Tower, charms dangling from it. A four-leaf clover and a roller skate were visible.

"She's very cute," said Sven, pointing to the picture. "That tiny bracelet looks like it could fit her."

"Thank you." Charles' voice softened, as did his eyes. "That's my daughter. She's away, but when she returns, I plan to give it to her. I always give her gifts when I travel." Charles cleared his throat and sat behind his desk in the corner, the only sound of the clock ticking across the room, which caught Charles' attention. "I don't have much time, but since you are already here, tell me, what's on your mind?" Sven sat across from him.

"I think that you building your company on the present land is a big mistake." He pulled out his launchpad and pointed to a white wall, the only blank wall in the room, and turned it on.

"Now this land would be better suited for what you are looking for." He flipped through the pictures of the land that he had found for sale on the other side of town, expansive and clear. "You wouldn't even have to bulldoze barely anything, and the foundation of the land is supposed to be solid. I checked."

"And where is this land?" Charles asked.

"Just on the other side of town. I have all the information for you if you would like, and the price is half the price of what you paid for your present land."

Charles leaned back in his chair, rubbing his chin. He narrowed his eyes.

*Maybe he was considering...*

"No."

"But, Mr. Williams, you haven't even looked at all of the information yet. Don't you want to think it over? It's a deal of a lifetime. You would save so much money." Sven didn't know if his blood pressure was rising from stress or frustration. *Why can't this man be reasonable? He's not even listening.* He fought the urge to yell out his thoughts.

Charles stood and reached out his hand to shake Sven's. "I appreciate all the effort you put into this, but I don't think it's the right fit for me. The other land I bought is the perfect location. This won't do. If you want to leave me the information on the other land, I might consider it for other business ventures in the future."

"And that's it? You're not even going to consider it?" Sven stood, his face tense, shoving the chair to the side a little too hard. It was on wheels and ran into the wall. The knickknacks and pictures shook.

Charles clenched his fists. "It is time for you to leave, Dr. Olander. You are no longer welcome in this house. It's bad enough you showed up on my land trying to stop the construction that is legal in every way. The next time you come back without an invitation from myself, I will call the proper authorities. As for today, I will escort you out."

"I apologize." Sven took a deep breath, trying to find the right words. He closed his launchpad and fumbled to switch it off, taking a couple of tries. Clenching his hands, his fingernails dug into his palms. Releasing them, his head throbbed and shoulders stiffened. "Do you see how this is a bad idea? We are talking about the future of the world. That tree is the only place on earth that has the tree frogs where they can make the serum from to cure the mutants. As you know, the serum is getting scarce. People are stealing it, getting hooked on it, and using it for something other than what it is supposed to do. Don't you get how this could affect the entire world?"

"I've known about the tree for some time now. I am assuming you spoke with the state? They paid me a visit during the construction, where I assured them it was nowhere near the tree." Charles narrowed his eyes. "I know you don't trust me, but that will lead to nothing but trouble."

Sven pressed his lips together as if it would stop him from speaking any other secrets. Had he said those words out loud? No! No! NO!

What Charles had said seeped in. Sven ignored Charles' threats. "You've known?"

"Of course. A rich and powerful man such as myself has many connections. As for the serum, there's plenty more where that came from," said Charles, urging Sven to go. "I know they have secret stashes everywhere. They just aren't sharing, so don't pull that shit on me. What's wrong with a little piece for myself? And do you know what I can do with what's on this land? I could improve lives, Doctor. Even your own."

Sven took a moment to speak, not trusting himself. "What could you ever do for me, besides get off the property?"

Charles smiled so big his white teeth glistened. "I know about your wife. What if you didn't have to lose her?"

Sven's mouth dropped. He sounded so absolute, like he knew what he was talking about. He can't be serious. Sven gave himself one minute to believe that he was telling the truth. He knew about the serum, that Sven was certain. Charles didn't react after Sven had told him. The thought of Hannah being back in his life, healthy and happy, the way that she was years ago, gave him a glimmer of hope. Money can do a lot of things, but it couldn't bring her back...could it? But could he ever trust this man?

"You aren't making any sense," Sven seethed in frustration. The man wasn't fighting fairly. With Hannah on his mind, he couldn't focus on why he came. "I need to go."

"Yes, go." Charles motioned for Sven to follow him. "Think about it."

Sven followed him out, not saying a word. At the same time, he wondered where the little girl could be. He didn't know a lot about Charles, but he never heard of a daughter. Charles flew open the door, literally throwing Sven out back into the garage.

# Chapter Eleven

Crickets chirped through the clear night. Moonlight shows through Sven's window, the only light in his bedroom, casting a shadow. He thought of what Charles had told him three days ago, and for three days, his frustration grew. He wondered about Charles' distrust for the police. Could it be because of his visit with Michael Stratford's associates? Every time he treated the mutants, he thought of how Charles could destroy them. Every time he thought of Hannah, he wondered if Charles could help. Sven clenched his fists so tight his knuckles were white. Charles knew about Hannah, but what could he do? Her removed hospital bed created grooves in the carpet where the footboard and headboard pressed. Kneeling down on the floor, he put his fingers in the indentations and thought that the room looked too big now. The empty space wasn't supposed to be so open.

"Got to go, hun. I have things to do. Wish me luck." He imagined her there, telling him to be safe and to put on warmer clothes. She was always worried he would catch a cold. Sweet Hannah.

The next step would be the garage. His toolbox was massive, and he opened the drawers of tools that he bought but barely used. Pristine condition. Perfect. The compartment on the bottom held larger tools, where he grabbed mallets, hammers, and gigantic Allen wrenches. Screwdrivers were in another drawer, and he put a handful in a knapsack that he could barely lift. *Damn, I'm getting old.*

Throwing everything in the trunk of his car, he checked his air pressure on all of his tires, his windows, mirrors, and lights. Just the thought of breaking down or missing a mutant in one of his mirrors before he hits it increased his caution. With shaking hands, he started the car via push button, his fingerprint making the indentation. What would happen if he ever lost an arm? He didn't like where his mind was going.

The motion sensors let him know it was safe to back up, so lifting the doors, he proceeded out into the street. Not used to driving this late at night, the time nearly midnight, he went to turn on some music, but decided against it. It was time for him to be focused on the task at hand.

"Well, I can't talk reason into the man," he said, "so I will just have to stop what he's doing in other ways. Or at least slow him down. Trusting him is not an option."

Clouds had rolled in, and even though there wasn't any rain, the world was pitch black except for the dim streetlights that ended as he exited town. Remembering the recent catastrophe that he had assisted, he kept his eyes focused on everything around him, and his headlights on bright.

He was fortunate. The night was quiet.

Sven wondered if Charles had the new fence built around the perimeter of the property to keep mutants out or himself. He parked far away from any area of his land and walked the rest of the way. Remembering the astute cameras that were on Charles' house, he covered his face in black with a ski mask, the newest kind that was warm as hell but easy to breathe through. All that anyone would see would be a shadow.

Sven hated to admit it, but he would be a great burglar.

He brought with him bolt cutters, brand new and top-of-the line, cutting through the fence like butter. It took him time to do this far enough so he could walk through, and he took a break when he got tired, but not too long. Someone, man or beast, could catch him, and he wasn't about ready to chance it.

When he made it through, he illuminated his flashlight all around the area, and sure enough, there were cameras pointing at all the equipment. *No need to destroy the cameras, just the power source.* He inched toward the wires that activated them and sniped them with no problem. Someone else may not have looked for them, but someone else didn't know Charles. Maybe they wouldn't notice the cut wires and thought the cameras were still storing information.

Now that was done, it was safe to pull his vehicle closer and empty the trunk. He pulled off his mask, backing up the BMW and taking out the largest hammer that he could. Going back through the hole in the chain-link fence, he sliced his shoulder as it got caught on a loose wire. "Damn." Blood drizzled out of the wound as he placed pressure on it. "I don't have time for this. It's just a scratch." He climbed onto the bulldozer, breaking the windows with hard blows.

He thought of Hannah, and the fact she wasn't there anymore with him. Anger welled up inside him and flowed through his arms, crashing into glass. It took many strikes before tiny shards exploded and spread. Keeping aware of everything around him at all times, he continued to shatter the glass. He broke the doors, yelling at the top of his lungs as he did it. No one was out there to hear him. Tears flowed down his face. "You asshole, you will not win!" Sven's clothes stuck to his skin in sweat. He found the screwdriver and undid every screw he could find as well as he could with trembling hands.

Getting into the engine, he cut every single wire he could. He smashed the battery into pieces with a hammer.

He continued to destroy the equipment, smashing and tearing as much as possible. A slight rain fell, making the metal slippery, and he slowed so he wouldn't fall. His labored breathing made his mind swim. Being hurt out here would not only be a long time for medical help, but his chances of being caught intensified.

Howling echoed in the distance. Damn, he had forgotten his tranquilizer gun in the car, sitting in the glove compartment. He hoped the creature was as far away as it sounded, but out in the woods sometimes it was hard to tell, especially in the dark and poor weather. Climbing off the machine, he caught himself while slipping. Ready to rush to the car on the other side of the fence when he could hear something or someone running in the distance. From the sound, it was more likely an animal, perhaps a mutant animal, of some sort. Almost falling off the excavator, squeezing through the hole in the fence he wished he would have made bigger, he sliced himself more than before, bleeding all the way to the car. Slamming the car door shut, he frantically went through his glove box until he pulled out the tranquilizer gun, wishing he had an actual gun. He promised himself a long time ago, it was all about saving the animals. What was he thinking?

A snarl came from outside the car, and it sounded dangerously close. A barking so loud it deafened him. How many were there? There had to be more than one.

Staring outside into the night, which he could barely see, he tried to prepare the tranquilizer gun, jumping when a mutant pounced against the window. Locking the door in panic, he shook his head. Like a mutant would know how to unlock a door. "Where there's one of you, there's usually more," he said, glad to be inside his car instead of out there in the woods. His breathing was erratic and his heart pounded as his ears rang.

The mutant was circling the car. The thing was on all fours, full of ratted fur with a protruded snout and a mouth underneath full of sharp teeth, dripping blood from a recent kill. Its legs were muscular and massive, ending in claws of various lengths. Deep-Set eyes shone bright in the darkness. Sven took in a sharp breath and panicked in the car, pushing up against his seat as if he could melt into the interior. A thump vibrated, like someone was getting in the back seat.

Impossible with the locked doors, but the trunk was open. Banging hard enough on the back of that back seat through the trunk, and it would surely collapse, and he would be in the car.

Sven flipped backward, starting at the back of the back seat, frantically doing what he had to do. He picked up the gun where he dropped it, unlocked the car door, and fell out, stepping wrong and his foot went sideways. His ankle was killing him, but that wouldn't be the only thing that was hurting if he didn't hurry. The creature continued to thump on the back of the truck, unaware that Sven had departed. The car rocked and the trunk closed with a snap.

If everything was closed, the wolf would be trapped in the car. Sven still had his car door wide open, and when he went to stand and shut it, his leg collapsed underneath him. Pain traveled up to his hip. Damn it! None of this was supposed to happen, and it was going so smoothly.

He put the tranquilizer dart in the gun, thankful he didn't have to get too close, and waited. He couldn't crawl away fast enough, and the car was his only way to get home. Besides, he knew he did enough damage to the property for one day to delay them on their work, and it might even make Charles think for a moment what he was doing and its effect on the world.

Or at least slow him down until Sven came up with another plan.

There was a crash and a thump from inside the car. The back seat folded down, and he could see the mutant in the cabin of the BMW. The leather seats were being torn to shreds as the wolf made it to the front of the car, where Sven was less than six feet away.

As soon as the animal made it out of the car, Sven shot a tranquilizer dart in its leg, and it howled, but didn't slow. Sven prepped another dart, at the same time trying to push himself farther away from the creature. The wolf hobbled, but still was moving toward him, and he shot again, the dart hitting his side. He knew he only had three left. Sven couldn't miss. He also knew they took longer to start taking effect for some mutants.

He might not have that kind of time.

The creature kept at Sven, and Sven scrambled up, hurt, sore, and tired, but his survival instinct kicked in. Somehow he could load these darts at lightning speed, and he hit the mutant again in the other leg. The thing was hobbling, but still moving, its gait slower.

But so had Sven's, and he didn't like the fact that he was moving away from his car, his only way to get away. He wished he would have brought something with him when he left the car in the first place, but he was so hell-bent on destruction, and look where it had gotten him.

"Leave me alone!" he tried to yell, but it came out as a whisper. As if the wolf could understand him, anyway. In frustration, he shot another dart, missing his target totally. "Damn it."

Sven fell on his back, but raised his head quick enough before it hit the hard earth, and his weapon flew out of his hands. Reaching to his right, it was too far to stretch to get his gun, and the mutant came at him almost in slow motion.

And collapsed on Sven.

That's when Sven realized he was holding his breath. He let it out and tried to push the animal off of him, taking several minutes. Sven dragged himself into the car's driver's side after picking up his tranquilizer gun and closing the trunk. His torn, muddy, bloody car smelled like a wet dog.

And he was so damn tired.

He drove away, the first time in a long time, without checking the tires, the lights, or the mirrors.

— · —

# CHAPTER TWELVE

Sven woke up to a loud banging on his front door. Exhausted, sore, and bloody, he dragged himself to answer without even checking his security, watch, or anything of the sort, he got off the couch to get it. He peered at the screen next to the door on the inside. Jesse. Christ.

"One second," Sven spat, trying to straighten his disheveled hair and hide some of his wounds. In only his boxer shorts and a t-shirt, he flung open the door. "What are you doing here, Jesse?"

"I know you called in," said Jesse, shaking his head. "I wanted to make sure that you were okay? You're obviously not."

"That's ridiculous. I'm fine." Sven went to close the door, but Jesse slid his foot in the way.

"Just let me in for a minute, will ya?" Reluctantly, Sven opened the door and shut it quickly behind him.

"See? I'm fine. I told you." Sven flopped in his nearby recliner. A cut oozed on his forehead and his leg stung where he was sure there were more abrasions. Bruises were tender to the touch, and he hadn't even taken a shower yet, so he was still filthy. There were mud tracks across his living room floor from the kitchen.

"What the hell happened to you? What have you been doing?"

"None of your goddamn business."

*Stupid kid. Get the hell out of my house.*

He thought about it, but he would never say it. Not to Jesse. All he wanted to do was go back to bed, and maybe clean up a bit, after he was feeling better. A nap was what he needed, not twenty questions.

"I'm worried about you," said Jesse, sitting on the end of the couch, leaning into Sven. "You're all cut up, and you're limping. Did you fall?"

"You think I'm some old man you have to take care of?" he asked. "I'm fine. I told you."

"We're friends. You can talk to me." Jesse looked down for a minute, then said, "You're like a dad to me, and I know you feel the same way. Don't pretend you don't."

"Forgive me for not cleaning up," said Sven, rolling his eyes. "I didn't know I was going to have company."

Jesse stood up and paced the floor. "What were you doing? Rolling around in the mud? Where did you go?" Jesse pointed to the front door. "You know it's not safe out there." Sven sat and stared at him, without saying a word. "You're not going to tell me? Look, I'm sorry for what happened, but you have to move on with your life."

"Don't." Sven was firm, and his whole body tensed. "Don't go there, do you hear me?" His head was swimming and he was fighting back tears. There was no reason. She wasn't gone forever, but frozen in time so one day she can awaken, like those old fairy tales. Sleeping Beauty. Trying to stay positive was exhausting.

"I think you should go clean up, and I can help you if you want me to with the dressings. You are going to need to put something on those, and then you can tell me where the hell you were. Jeez, Sven, you would say the same thing to me."

"No, I don't need your help. I need you to leave. Sometimes a man needs to be by himself. I called in from work because I wasn't feeling well, and I didn't lie. I don't feel well. I need rest."

"Okay," said Jesse, standing up to leave. "But you know I will be back if you're still here tomorrow. You can't hide in here."

"I know." Sven paused, eager to change the subject. "How are you?" Sven knew he looked horrible himself, but he knew why. Jesse was paler than normal, and there was less energy in his step.

"I'm okay." He shrugged. "I just haven't been sleeping well."

"Follow me." *Yes, someone to take care of. I have missed this.* Sven opened up a cabinet above the stove, pulling out a canister clear with green herbs in it. "This makes a great tea that will help you sleep."

"I don't really think—" Jesse began.

"Take it." Sven thrust it out in front of him, and Jesse tucked it under his arm.

"Okay," he said. "Thanks."

"Now, Jesse, you go home and get a good night's sleep, and I will see you tomorrow. We will both be looking better."

Jesse gave him a smile.

"Sorry if I said the wrong thing."

"No apologies," said Sven. "We're all just doing the best that we can, right? And you leave by the garage door. It's safer. Where did you park?"

"Just in front of the house. It's fine. It's getting better, remember?"

Sven narrowed his eyes at him. "Not totally, young man. You still need to be cautious." Jesse pulled a spidomed from his pocket, a mini version an inch around with the safety cap on. "Well, at least that's something. Is it pre-filled with something potent?"

"Oh, yeah," said Jesse. "I always try to be prepared."

"Good. All the same, I think I'll keep an eye on you until you get to the car. Just give me a moment. I'll start the old coffee pot so Hannah and I can have our afternoon coffee." Sven grasped the coffee from the cupboard, clutching it in his fists. Two creams, two sugars. Half a cup of milk. Hannah loved her coffee sweet. Jesse was quiet behind him in words and movements. It was so much easier to imagine her upstairs taking a nap or watching television. She would come down the stairs, stretching her long arms to the sky before they wrapped around him.

"I smell coffee," she would say with a smile before she planted a kiss on his cheek. "Time for Pinochle. Where are the potato chips, darling?"

Sven didn't have many days off, but when he did, it was cards, coffee, and chips. Sometimes they would invite the neighbors over.

Sven flipped around to see Jesse staring at him with puzzlement, then his gaze traveling to avoid Sven. He started some coffee. "She's here in her own way," he said, pulling out two coffee cups. "Want some?"

"Sure," said Jesse as his stomach rumbled.

Sven noticed he was getting a little hungry himself. "Want a bite to eat instead?"

"I wouldn't dream of you hobbling around the kitchen for me," said Jesse.

"I'm hungry. Just give me a few minutes, will you? You can help, so I won't be hobbling around, as you say," Sven said, putting the coffee back in the cupboard. *I lied to Jesse. I don't want to be by myself in my own thoughts. At least this will give me something else to think about, and I am hungry.*

"Stew or chili?" asked Jesse, knowing they were two of Sven's specialties.

"Funny you should mention that. I have some leftover stew in the fridge, and since I'm starving, I'm going to take a shortcut with the thermo-bag…"

"Sit," said Jesse. "Just tell me where the stuff is, and I'll do it."

Sven stuck a Milky Way in his mouth after unwrapping it from his goodie drawer. "I got the appetizer."

Jesse moved with ease around the kitchen after washing his hands with precision, as only a doctor would do. He helped Sven many times before on get-togethers they had throughout the years working as a team and knew where everything was. Jesse sang while getting the bowls from the cupboard. In less than a minute, he had two steaming bowls of stew in front of them and ice tea.

"All that I could find to drink in the fridge," said Jesse.

"I haven't gone to the store." Sven took in the aroma of the stew consisting of carrots, potatoes, and huge hunks of tender beef that melted in his mouth as he ate. It dawned on him he hadn't eaten for longer than he could recall. "Thanks for coming over." He put his hand on Jesse's shoulder.

"Sure. Thank you for having leftovers." The two men ate in silence, and then Jesse broke it. "I'm serious. You don't look well."

"I'm more worried about you. You look way too pale. Have you been losing weight?"

Jesse laughed. "If I keep eating like this, I won't have to worry about that at all. Nah, I'm all right. Just working a lot, I guess, but that's nothing new."

"Why don't you take some home?" Sven said.

"As long as you let me take you shopping or at least bring some more food in your house. The cupboards are looking a little bare."

"Deal." Sven stood and felt like he was about ready to collapse. "I hate to bring this up, but could you do me a favor and not mention this to anyone else? I don't want them to think I have lost my mind."

"Yeah, it is weird to see you not clean," said Jesse. "I won't say anything more today, but I'm keeping an eye on you."

Sven walked him toward the garage, checking all the motion detectors for safety. After the door opened, Jesse in front of him, he heard a "my God, Sven, what the hell happened to your car?"

"Oh, shit," he said. "The strangest thing happened..." Sven couldn't think of an excuse. He was too tired, physically and mentally. Definitely emotionally. And he wasn't ready to make something up. Sven sat on the step that goes out to the garage while Jesse made his way around the outside of the car, gawking at every dent, scratch, broken window, and busted latch. He ran his hand over the once perfect paint job, and the scrunched up expression made Sven wince.

Sven always kept his car spotless, tuned up, charged, and in pristine condition. To see it so mangled again just reminded him of what happened, and why it was like that. It was Charles.

Everything was his fault.

"Were you attacked by a mutant? I don't understand. You're always so careful. Where did this happen? If you were in a car accident this severe, I would assume you would be in worse shape than you are now." Jesse eyed Sven up and down. "Are there any other injuries?" He let out a heavy breath. "You haven't told me, why, what actually happened?"

"I was kind of in the woods, and I kind of got attacked by a mutant. Well, almost attacked by a mutant. I tranquilized him before he could get to me."

"Why didn't you tranquilize it right away?"

Sven let out a groan.

"I am not leaving until you give me more than just you felt like taking a walk in the woods and a mutant chased you? I don't believe you."

"Jesse..." Sven stood and winced. His body was so sore and he was exhausted.

"Here, let me help you inside," said Jesse, taking Sven's arm as they retreated back into the house. "I'll help you with these sores and at least check you for broken bones."

"I'm a doctor. I think I would know if something was broken," he yelled.

"I won't let you do that." Jesse continued to help Sven back into the house. "I won't let you push me away. Why don't you go up and take a shower, and I'll help you with all the dressings?"

"Fine. Just so you'll leave me alone." Sven made it through the kitchen and almost collapsed, going into the living room. "I just need to sit for a minute." He cozied up in his recliner.

"Tell me what happened, and I will leave you alone. Are you sleepwalking? Is there something that you're looking for? Someone?"

The questions rang in Sven's mind. Why did Jesse have to come over today of all days?

"Does this have something to do with the tree of life?" Sven's eyes grew enormous for one second, and he bowed his head to avoid Jesse seeing his expression. "I know you were out there when you found the construction site. You were telling us all about it at work. You went back there, didn't you? Did you have a fight with that Williams character?" Jesse sat at the end of the couch. "But nothing would tear apart you or your car like that...except, maybe a mutant, *like you said.*"

*Good Lord, this kid is smart, and close enough, so I might as well tell him. He's going to put it together, anyway.*

"Yes, Jesse, I went out there." Jesse stayed still, listening intently. "I have no intention of letting that man get in the way of making this world a better place by building his crap all over the land that is going to save the world, so I may have destroyed some machinery and some cameras. That mutant caught me off guard. I didn't have my tranquilizer gun. It was in the glove box. I ran to get it, but the mutant made his way into my car from the back." Jesse narrowed his eyes, and Sven raised up his hands.

"True story."

*God, my shoulders hurt.*

"Sven…" Jesse stopped. "I believe you. Finally, you told me the truth. You should have told me."

"You would have stopped me."

"That's not the point. I was watching all the footage from those security cameras. I hacked into his security company, but now I have nothing. It must have been when you destroyed the wires." Jesse shook his head. "A damn shame."

"I didn't know." Sven shrugged before narrowing his eyes and pointing his finger at Jesse. "You should have told me."

"I thought you were going through enough and didn't want to say anything until I knew it worked, trying to make the best out of my electronics minor. Let's make a deal. You don't go out on your own and bust up equipment by yourself, where you are likely to get hurt, and I will let you know my plan of attack. Sometimes a distant approach is safer. Deal?"

"What do I get out of the deal?" asked Sven. "What will you promise me?"

"You will get a kickass doctor for the day. So, when you're ready, I will help you to the shower, unless you think you need help." Sven gave him a cold stare.

"I have a chair in there, so I'll be just fine."

"Oh, of course, because of—" He stopped mid-sentence, his eyes downcast and mouth still agape.

"You can say her name. Yes, because of Hannah." Oh, how he missed her. She would know exactly what to do.

*Why did she have to get sick? Why did she have to leave me? For now. Just for now.*

Stopping the tears, the boulder in his stomach swelled as did his throat. Unable to breathe, Jesse watched him, then said, "Sven, don't. You don't have to do it for me. Let it out."

But Sven refused to cry for someone that was going to come back to him someday. "I'm going to take a shower before you get all sappy on me," and he made his way to the bathroom.

—·—

## CHAPTER THIRTEEN

"I'm sorry it took so long," said Nathan on the other end of the line. Sven stared at his nephew through the computer screen. It had been such a long time; he had almost forgotten the child had grown up. "I'll be there in a few minutes. How are you doing?"

"Fine," Sven lied. He had the lights dim in his bedroom as he talked to Nathan, his abrasions almost non-existent in the shadows. The monitor was dim as well, making Sven look more like a shadow than his actual face. He was still trying to figure out what he was going to tell him when he arrived, and he had little time.

"Okay," said Nathan, seemingly unconvinced. "I'll be there in a few minutes." And the screen went black.

Sven went into the bathroom and looked at himself in the mirror with the blinding lights on him. He washed his face, wincing at the pain. Opening up the medicine cabinet, he found bottles of pills, gauze, and expired night cream that was Hannah's. Cover up blemishes? Unscrewing the jar, he put a little on his face, instantly stinging where the jaw was swelling. There was no way he was going to hide his bruising. Nathan wasn't an idiot. There wasn't a lot any kind of concealer could do at this point.

Jumping on the computer, knowing he had some time, he re-investigated Charles' property line. Narrowing his eyes, he leaned into the screen. It appeared the property no longer included the land that held the tree of life. The acreage had shrunk considerably.

The doorbell rang, and Sven hit the button on his view master on the wall in his room. "Yeah, Nathan, come on in." He could hear the door slam, and watched Nathan enter the house, putting down his overnight bags. Flipping off the computer, he headed down the stairs. Nathan stood awkwardly until Sven came into view. "Thank you, Nathan, for coming."

"Of course." Nathan reached out to Sven and hugged him hard for a full minute before pulling away. He still held onto him by his shoulders and inspected him. "Uncle Sven, you look horrible."

"It's a long story."

"Do you still have that great hot chocolate? Maybe we could sit and talk about it." Sven smiled, remembering when Nathan was a boy and they would sit in the kitchen and drink hot chocolate. They played cards and talked about school and friends. He was always the cool Uncle Sven that was a genius. Nathan, at one time, wanted to be just like him.

Then he grew up into his own man.

"Let me show you where you'll be sleeping," said Sven, about ready to lead him to his room.

"Don't worry, I remember."

"Right..." he hesitated. Of course he remembered; it was the same house he'd grown up visiting. "I'll just...start the cocoa, then," said Sven, watching Nathan walk to the back of the house. Sven put some hot water on the stove. He knew there were faster ways, but sometimes something was to be said for tradition and patience. The hot cocoa packets were next to the stove. Nathan had gotten older. How long has it been? He had grown into a man with beard stubble and a crew cut. His baby face was gone, his expression hard. Maybe he was sad, too.

*You weren't the only one that lost her.*

Sven, being the only one left of eight brothers and sisters, he thought of how fast the family was shrinking. I must save Hannah.

Lost in thought, he didn't even notice when Nathan entered the kitchen and pulled up a chair at the table. "You always made the greatest cocoa," he said. "What do you need help with? I am here to help."

"Help? It's nice that you came to visit, but don't worry. I don't need help with anything."

"Obviously you do." Nathan stood and walked over to Sven. "You don't have to be a cop to notice when something is wrong, and I mean seriously wrong. What happened to you? Were you attacked?"

"You know how dangerous the world is." The teakettle whistled, breaking the silence between them. Sven poured the chocolate into the mugs, pouring the hot water over them and stirring. "Do you still like whipped cream?"

"Don't change the subject. Yes, I'll get it." Nathan turned to the fridge, but still kept talking to Sven. "You need to tell me what is going on. What happened to you?"

"A mutant almost attacked me, if you need to know the truth," said Sven. *I'm not lying.*

"Where were you almost attacked? You are one of the most careful people I know."

"Wrong place, wrong time." Sven tried to shrug it off, but Nathan wasn't buying it. "Okay, I was going for a walk in a place I shouldn't have. I probably wasn't thinking. I've had a lot on my mind."

"The important thing is that you're okay. I'm sorry, I shouldn't have interrogated you like that. I guess I'm used to it with the job and everything, but I'm not here as a cop." Nathan loaded up his cocoa with whipped cream before taking a sip. His eyes rolled backward and he smiled. "I sure missed you, Uncle Sven." Sven smiled at him and drank his own hot cocoa. "Look, a smile." Nathan rubbed his hands on his pants, then wrapped them around the steaming mug again. "Is Aunt Hannah going to be buried in the family plot beside Lucas? Or has she already?

I want to see her and pay my respects." His eyes roamed the kitchen. "It's so strange not having her here."

"No, she's not." Sven cleared his throat and looked over at the man. "She's in a cryogenic state right now, just on the other side of town."

Nathan choked and pushed the cocoa away, almost spitting out what was in his mouth. "What did you do to her?"

"I did nothing bad to her, and don't talk to me like that. She's my wife, and it's my decision." *I knew he wouldn't understand, but it was going to come out, eventually. Best get it over with. No one is going to understand unless they go through it. Unless they are me.*

Nathan scooted his chair until he was right next to Sven. Sven could feel his breath on the nape of his neck. "She's gone."

Sven looked straight into his eyes. "For now."

"No, she's gone, and she's not coming back. Not on this earth."

"They are coming up with cures for everything all the time. We found a cure for mutations, for God's sake." Sven crossed his arms. He didn't want to talk about this anymore. Tired and stressed, his body aching from his run in with the mutant, and his pain meds were wearing off.

"We will never find a cure for death. No one is supposed to be here forever."

Sven's heart pounded. He stood and threw the cup in the sink, the mug breaking and shattering against the stainless steel. Nathan jumped, but stayed perfectly still.

"I'm going to bed," announced Sven. "I need my rest before something happens. As you say, no one is supposed to be here forever." He paused at the archway between the living room and kitchen, glancing behind him. "If I don't find a cure soon, you won't be visiting me at this house either. I plan on joining her at the cryogenics facility at the beginning of next year."

"But Uncle Sven, you can't do that unless you are..." Nathan stopped, swallowing a lump in his throat.

"Yes, I know. I don't plan to be alive when it takes place. I would leave you the house to take care of, but I assume you wouldn't want to relocate."

"I don't care about the house. I care about you."

"Then you will respect my decision, and I no longer wish to discuss this. I made up my mind, and I am tired. You change your tune, or I expect you to be gone in the morning."

"Uncle Sven, I'm sorry." Sven lifted his hand beside him, just wanting quiet. "I'll see you in the morning."

# Chapter Fourteen

Sven got up to his watch beeping. When he looked over and thought it was his alarm, he noticed someone was calling. Unfamiliar number.

"Hello?" Just waking up his voice was crackly. "Who is this? Can I help you?" He bolted up in bed. Was there an emergency at the hospital or with one of the boys?

"Dr. Olander? I'm sorry if I woke you." Charles' face filled the screen, and Sven tried to straighten his hair. "You don't look so well."

"I'm fine," he snapped.

"I would like to discuss something with you in person." *Maybe he has more information for me. What did he mean if I didn't have to lose Hannah? He has something brewing and I am going to find out what it is.* Sven stretched and got out of bed, placing the watch on his wrist. "Would you like to meet at my house, perhaps for lunch?"

"That would work."

"I will see you at noon then." Charles disconnected the call.

Abrupt. It doesn't matter. Sven began rifling through his clothes to find something to wear when he heard a noise downstairs. Nathan. He wouldn't understand any of this. He found a navy blue suit wedged in the back. Dusting it off, he laid it on the bed and prayed that it still fit, amazed that it was still together. He took a hot shower, wincing at the pain of water in his sores, but the steam and the water soothed his sore muscles.

Looking in the mirror, he combed his hair and stared at his reflection, looking back at him. Bloodshot eyes and a few scrapes, but nothing too drastic. He re-slathered miracle goo on his sores, which were sure to look better in a couple of hours and beat the obviousness of a bandage. Eye drops would take the redness out and he would be ready for his meeting.

His meeting. Biting his bottom lip, he wondered what Charles was going to say. So far, he hadn't been able to make any headway. What was the change of heart? Did he know that he was the one to destroy the equipment on his newfound property? Nah. If he did, he would have called the police and that would have been it. He wouldn't have wanted to talk.

"Uncle Sven," he heard from the kitchen. "I made coffee and pancakes."

"Perfect," said Sven with a smile. "Now let's see if his pancakes are as good as mine." Maybe things are going to be looking up for a minute. At least for this morning. "Just let me get dressed," he called down the stairs.

The pants were a little snug. With a button extender, he could button them, but the shirt and jacket fit okay. The white dress shirt stretched over his belly, so he found a sharp-looking blue tie with a swirly pattern to distract attention. A business meeting. It was nice to not be wearing this suit to a funeral. But then there were all the weddings.

"I wonder if Jesse is ever going to get married, or my own nephew, for that matter. He's such a workaholic." He looked in the mirror as he combed his hair.

*It does run in the family, I suppose.*

"Come on, it's getting cold," urged Nathan.

"One second."

As Sven neared the kitchen, the aroma drew him in. The coffee was strong, the smell of blueberry pancakes tickled his nose, and the sweet syrup. "Thanks, Nathan. You didn't have to..."

"Sit," Nathan said. All showered and dressed doing all this already, Sven wondered how long he had been pattering around the house, waiting for Sven to get up. Nathan poured coffee for Sven, handing him the creamer and a bowl of sugar cubes. "Yes, I remember how you like your coffee. A bit of coffee, lots of sugar."

"I don't put that much sugar in it," Sven replied, pouring in the creamer and adding four lumps of sugar. He stirred and sipped, adding two more lumps of sugar. Sipped. Perfection.

"Where did you learn to cook?"

"From my uncle. I remember when I was little and used to come over to your house. Aunt Hannah would be out in the garden or reading a book and you would be in here working on some perfect combination of ingredients to make the best chili or fancy fudge." He looked around the kitchen. "What happened to all the goodies?"

"I've been busy." He pointed to his goodie drawer. "You can help yourself, but don't go crazy."

Nathan placed the pancakes in front of Sven with a carafe of syrup freshly warmed.

"You look nice," said Nathan. "I didn't know you wore THAT suit to work. You always said it was under your lab coat anyway, so you kept the good stuff in good condition."

"I have a meeting today at noon. I'm sorry I can't stay here today and visit with you, but it's a very important meeting."

"I see. What's it about?"

Sven piled on the syrup and dug into his breakfast. The blueberries and syrup were a dynamic combination and he made an ummmm sound. "It's for work. You wouldn't be interested."

"That's okay. I can keep myself busy for one meeting. I'm glad you like breakfast."

"Delicious."

"Good. I think after the meeting you and I need to have a talk. To reconsider." Sven put down his fork with a clank and looked up at Nathan. Stared at him like lasers going through him. "I think Aunt Hannah shouldn't be at that place, and neither should you."

"Your Aunt will come back to you someday. Don't you want her back? Don't you love and miss her?"

Nathan pushed his lips together and rubbed his chin, averting Sven's gaze. "I'll always love and miss her. It would be amazing if she was here, but she went through so much. I would hate for her to go through all of that again. I can't stand the thought of losing both of you." Looking up at Sven again, he said, "Don't you agree?"

Sven's eyes lit up. "But that's just it. What if we found a cure for her condition? She wouldn't be in pain. She would be healthy and it could be like it once was. You have to see my point of view. They are finding cures all the time for things. We found a cure for the mutants."

"And look how well that is working out." Nathan points to all of Sven's wounds. "Look, I understand your point of view. I just don't agree with it. We all have our time. I'm sorry this is so hard to accept." Nathan's temple throbbed. "Why won't you listen to me?"

"Why won't you listen to me?" Sven stood up. "You're trying to ruin everything."

Nathan stood, feet spread and planted on the ground, hands clenching the table. "I am trying to help." Now it was Nathan's turn to throw things. "I love you, but I won't take this. You won't listen to reason. It's bad enough where Aunt Hannah is.

You're just going to do what you want, and I will have no part in watching you kill yourself. I came up here when I was in a major case at work and passed it on to the next guy, so I could be here with you."

"Sorry to inconvenience you." Sven pushed his plate away. "I'm not hungry. Besides, I don't want to get anything on my suit. I better go prepare for my meeting. Have a safe trip home." Sven returned to his bedroom. *I am done talking to Nathan. I don't need anything prepared to talk to Charles, because I just need to remember my speech before. He must have thought about it and saw something in it. It was the perfect excuse to leave. I don't want to fight.*

Sven sat on the edge of the bed and glanced at his watch. He had time before his meeting to at least help Nathan with dishes. Maybe now he understood not to talk about it. *I have made my decision and I am not going to change it.*

Sven waited for about fifteen minutes, just gathering his energy. Glancing over to where Hannah used to lie, he thought about putting something there. It was a vacant spot, and she left a vacant spot where he didn't want to be reminded. Maybe if he could go to the Cryonic lab to see where she was, it would make him feel better. Maybe after the meeting.

For now, he was ready to talk to Nathan. Leaning on his knees, he got up and jumped when he heard the front door slam.

"Safe journey," Sven said. *At least he didn't go through the garage; then I'd have more explaining to do. He* thought of his once beautiful BMW, now dented and scratched beyond recognition. "There's no way I can drive that to Charles'. I must find another way." He thought of his backup car. He hadn't driven it in a long time, but it would just have to work.

# CHAPTER FIFTEEN

Sven pulled out of the garage one hour later in a red car that could barely fit him. The sprint was one of the earliest electric cars with no bells and whistles, sitting in his garage for years. He had just finished re-charging it, and grumbled, turning around to look behind him. He had checked the lights twice, mirrors, and battery. "Damn mutant," he muttered, pulling out when the sensors declared it was safe.

Classical music played out of the radio, and his grip on the steering wheel loosened as he listened. What would this man expect of him? He would give everything he had to have his Hannah back. Live in a cardboard box forced to eat garbanzo beans for the rest of his days. Sven hated the infernal beans, forced to eat them when he was young and his parents were scraping by. But for Hannah, he would eat all the garbanzo beans in the world.

Pulling in front of Charles' mansion, he hoped this visit went better than his last. He went through the same way, the garage, and Charles appeared on the screen next to the door.

It surprised Sven that it wasn't one of his staff. Charles was smiling, and he looked different. The smile transformed the man, increasing his appeal significantly.

*Tread carefully. You can't trust him.*

"Come in," said Charles, Max at his heels. The door unlocked and opened on its own accord. Sven stepped through and followed Charles. "I am so sorry for what happened before. You were right. It's time that we talk like two grown men that can help each other."

Sven wondered what kind of heart Charles possessed.

"I apologize for losing my temper. Control is key in all situations. If we lose our control, we can lose so much."

*What can he want from me?*

They made it to Charles' dining room, or at least one of them. The table wasn't as extensive as Sven would have thought, but this was only the smaller of others. It sat four with two place settings for lunch. The oak table had intricately designed legs of flowers and wildlife. The corner where he saw a wolf's face made him shutter. Did this man have control of all things, even the local wildlife? No, Sven, you are thinking nonsense.

"I hope you like duck," said Charles, "in black cherry sauce. It's my favorite."

"Yes, duck is fine." Sven couldn't remember the last time he had such a luxury. He sipped on the poured wine. It was important to keep his wits about him and his mind clear.

"I normally do my business in my office, but business of this nature, I thought it was more fitting in a casual setting." Sven wondered how talking of real estate was fitting of a more casual setting, but merely nodded and went along with it. As Charles sipped on his wine as well, Max stayed at his master's side. He didn't bark or barely move, and Charles leaned down to pet the dog.

"He's so well-behaved," said Sven. "A beautiful dog."

"He's a part of the family," said Charles. "If anything were to happen to Max, I don't know what I would do." His brown eyes darkened and almost turned a crimson red. "Do we have an understanding?"

Sven pulled his head back and shook it, a sour expression filling his face. "Frankly, I'm a little offended. I would never hurt a defenseless animal. I think you forgot I spend most of my time healing them. If my life was in danger..."

"You work with mutants, doctor."

"Yes, they are animals with medical problems that aren't their fault." *The nerve of this man. Let's cut to the chase before he says another asinine thing.* Veins pulsed on his neck. "So, why don't you tell me why you called me here today?"

"Patience." A slender woman came out in an apron and flowery dress. Her nails were short and clean, along with the rest of her. She served the duck without a word, placing everything on the table.

"Is there anything else?"

"We're fine, Marcy." He dismissed her with a brush of his hand, and Sven smiled at her. "I brought you here today to help you. I help you and you help me." Charles cut into his duck and took a bite. Sven stared at the duck, which looked delicious, and wondered if he was being poisoned. Absurd. All the same, he cut off a couple of pieces and pushed them around on his plate.

Charles laughed at him, switching their plates. "The food is perfectly fine. Take mine. What, you thought I was going to poison you?"

Sven raised his eyebrows and said, "Of course not." He shook his head and took a bite, moaning at the delicious taste that filled his mouth.

"What would you say if I told you I had the key to life?"

Sven's duck slipped down his throat before he could chew, throwing him into a coughing fit. He thought of when Charles said Sven might not have to lose Hannah, then his mind went to the tree on his property, and he grew nervous. After taking a sip of water, he said, "Why did you call me here today? Do you plan on answering my question I asked at our last meeting? What could you do for me?" Opening his arms wide in a grand gesture, he tried to remind himself to tread lightly, but he couldn't help the roughness in his tone.

"Now, calm down and don't jump to conclusions," said Charles.

Max whimpered.

"He doesn't like tension. Lower your tone and let me finish." Charles snickered. "I can barely enjoy my lunch."

Sven felt like a kid scolded at the dinner table, and here he was, decades older than this man. "Sorry."

"I know what you did. I'm not an idiot. You destroyed a lot of property, trespassing, and set our construction back for days, perhaps longer. I could have you arrested." Sven almost choked and took a sip of water. "But I didn't. Not yet. Maybe we could make a deal where both of us could be happy. Your end of the bargain would include never setting foot on that property again unless invited, and you don't get in my way of doing what I want to do on my property. Come to think of it, I don't have to make a plan with you at all, considering it is MY property." Charles took a small piece of duck and put it under the table for Max. He took it gingerly from his owner and savored it just as much as the two men did. "But you have something that I need." Charles took a bite of duck, a sip of wine, and it was an endless pause.

"So, what is your big idea? What are you offering me?" Sven stared into those deep eyes, not wavering. If Charles was lying, he was sure to know it.

"What would you say if I told you I could bring your wife back to you?" Sven paused, perplexed. "And with all of your medical knowledge, you can help me."

"There's no way you could do that...." Sven was trembling and babbling from shock. "Some day, but not yet. How would you know?"

Charles cleared his throat in warning. "I have some of the serum. I own one of the biggest pharmaceuticals in the Pacific Northwest, of course I have the serum. We have been experimenting with it. Dr. Olander, we have found that with some added ingredients and a stronger concentration, the serum could bring dead things back to the living."

Sven dropped his fork again. Could he be telling the truth? This man sitting across from him could bring back his Hannah? Why wouldn't it be anywhere else? The whole world had a right to know.

"No, I don't believe you." He eyed him skeptically. *The man had no proof.*

Charles seemed to read his mind and said, "It's not proven yet, but that doesn't mean it isn't a possibility. I have built my pharmaceutical company from the ground up and I expect to make great strides in progress." Charles straightened his back and lifted his chin. With a faraway look in his eyes, he said, "The local news will astound my brother and sister when they see it. I know Hannah Olander is in the Cryonic facility here in town, and I have the power to bring her back if you cooperate with me."

"Seriously?"

"Of course. I know most of the business owners in town. Fred and I just went scuba diving last year." Charles grinned.

"Isn't that a little reckless?" *With the pollution in the water, who knows how much of the virus they haven't truly contained? We can't filter the entire ocean.*

"What's life with a few risks?" Raising his eyebrows, he said, "I let Fred go first, of course." *Of course, thought Sven. Control is key.* He scoffed at his own thoughts. He didn't know Fredrick DeMarco well, but after speaking to him when he purchased a spot for both Hannah and himself, he seemed like a genuinely good man, as much as you could tell in that short a time. And he owns the facility. The air became cooler around Sven, and he was getting dizzy. The pain pills that he had taken that morning were wearing off. And shock. Could he have his Hannah back? If he didn't play nice with Charles, could Charles do something unforgivable to her before Sven got the chance?

He thought of her smile as she turned to him in bed in the morning. Memories of them when they first met taking trips to the beach, before the world got so horrible. Breakfast in bed on Sunday mornings, working together when the world changed. Installing new windows, watching out for each other and learning how to use every weapon in the book, adapting to a new world, they still held memories of the old. The pit in his stomach returned as he fought tears from missing her.

"I would need proof."

"I can't get you proof. I told you; we are still working on it. But if there was just a chance, aren't you going to take it?"

"You can at least show me what you have so far. You said you've been working on it."

"I don't have any of it with me. Everything is being done at the pharmaceutical company, and our finds are always changing. Now, you've known about the serum from the beginning. Am I right?"

"Yes..." Sven hesitated, not wanting to say too much again. "Actually, I've also been working with the mutants from almost the very beginning. Give me something, the latest findings if you will, and if you do find a way..." Bile rose in his throat as he swallowed. "And IF I agree to this, she won't be the first. This has to be proven. I won't have her come back not right." Sven took a deep breath to calm his nerves.

"That is fair, Dr. Olander. I will gather up what we have and we shall have another meeting."

Sven took another nibble of his duck, praying he wasn't being poisoned. The thought made him spit it out in his napkin. But what about the tree? Is he going to take all of the frogs, all of the source of the serum? We are talking about the end of the world. Everything would go to chaos, worse than before with all the mutants. They are already escalating because of the addicts taking the serum. We barely have enough as it is. It was almost to the point where someone could take a walk outside. Armed maybe, but they didn't have to resort to a covered, protected area with walls and electric fences.

Charles leaned in to Sven, putting his fork down and taking a sip of wine. They were eye to eye, and there was no way Sven could pull his gaze away. "Do you love Hannah?"

A blow to the gut. Sven shook, and his mouth dropped. His eyes narrowed into fine slits, and he said to him, "Don't you EVER question that I love her. I love her more than life itself. I love her more than myself. I don't know how I am going to get through the rest of my life without her."

"There's the question," said Charles. "Are you willing to live in a world less than perfect with her, or a perfect world without her?"

Sven froze. How dare he make such promises, but as he said, they weren't promises. They were possibilities. But at what cost? What kind of destruction could Charles do in the meantime?

"Give me some progress notes, and we will talk." Sven croaked. He couldn't believe he was even thinking about making a deal with the devil, but what he was offering was an opportunity of a lifetime. Narrowing his eyes and with a tilt of the head asked, "What's in it for you?"

"Are you kidding me?" Charles threw his head back and laughed. "If I could bring people back from the dead, that would make me the most powerful man on the planet. Control is key, and I will have complete control of everything." His eyes lit and widened, sparks behind the brown irises, introducing flecks of gold. "I figured we could help each other, but if you need something more concrete, I understand. I trust there will be no unwelcome visitations on my property until I gather the information?" He pointed to Sven's bruised face, and as much as Sven tried to cover it, the discoloration and bruising were obvious. Medicine has made leaps and bounds, but not miracles.

"No unwelcome visitors by anyone I know," remarked Sven. "Now if you will please excuse me, I must get home. I have a visitor from out of town. Family."

"Of course," said Charles, pulling his chair out to walk Sven to the door. "I am sure you will have a lot of decision-making to do. And there's one other stipulation."

"What's that?" *Like this couldn't get any more stressful.*

"This stays between you and me. You tell anyone what I am planning, all bets are off. No deal. You tell anyone, you set foot on my home without an invitation, on my newly acquired land without my prior knowledge, and I will end you. Your friends, the little family you have left, will pay. You will go to prison for a long time. I will think of something. Do we have an understanding?"

"Yes." Sven followed him back to the front, got into the garage, and Charles was gone. Slamming his fists on the steering wheel, the pain reverberated down his arms, sore from his earlier escapade. His ears rang at crazy decibels and his head pounded. What had he just done?

*Agreed to nothing. No one was in danger. Not yet. What am I to do? I can't lose Hannah forever, but do I have to wait until someone else finds a cure while she is frozen? I might be able to get her back before my hands are tied, before I have the chamber next to her. Charles won't be too hasty. I may have answers to his biggest questions about the serum.*

Sven jumped when the door to the garage opened. He knew Charles was watching on his monitor, seeing Sven slam his fists into the steering wheel, and that infuriated him further. Driving down the road, he wondered, what was the right road to take?

# Chapter Sixteen

Sven had called Nathan three times, with no answer. He hated how he had left things, but Nathan had to understand the stress he had been under. Sven just wanted to tell him he loved him. There were no guarantees of what was to happen in life, and he made himself that promise a long time ago.

He sat on the edge of the bed, looking over to where Hannah had slept next to him for so many years. Changing his mind about going to the cryonics facility because he wanted to remember her the way she was, the empty space not helping much. "I miss you, Hannah," he said. "I know you left me, and I know there was nothing you could do. It wasn't your fault." His face crinkled up in contemplation. "I am not sure what I am supposed to do. I miss you so much. I just want you back." He clutched the edge of the covers in tight fists. "I love you, Hannah. What am I supposed to do? I wish you were here to tell me. We were always a team, right?"

He sighed, knowing now was the time to face the music. He put more salve on his face after washing it. This new cream was supposed to heal wounds faster. His physical body was the least of his pain. As he drove to Juniper Ridge, he wondered how much Jesse had told the others at the facility. Jesse was never much of a gossiper, but he knew others would be asking, and Jesse would want to put their minds at ease.

Scanning his badge, using the fingerprint scanner to get in, he could feel the security guard watching him. "Dr. Olander," he nodded and watched him walk toward the main hallway.

Sven stopped and flipped around. "What is it, Tom? Is there anything you want to say to me?"

"Are you okay?"

Sven's face softened. "I'll be okay. Thank you for asking."

"Sure, Dr. O." As Sven continued down the hall, he couldn't help but remember there are still good people in this world that care, and it's all worth it. Someday the world will be like it was before when he was a boy, or at least as safe. He chuckled. If someone would have brought up teleportation fifty years ago, he would have laughed in their faces. Now look at them. They could teleport people, but they couldn't destroy a virus that surrounded the world. They would save everyone, and he was going to make damn sure of it.

And he was getting his Hannah back. He was going to make sure of that, too.

Doing both, that's what he wasn't sure of.

Broken out of his thoughts, Adam passed him in the hall. "Sven, could you do me a favor?" Adam paused at his rugged appearance, but didn't say a word about it. "I need to stop by Julia's room for an assessment. I could use the extra hand."

"Okay." Sven followed him to Julia's room. Julia had been a mutant at the Juniper Ridge facility for years. One side of her face appeared like she was in a fire and her eyes glowed an eerie green. She could see things and feel things. They had been giving her the serum and his anxiety rose to see how all of that had changed.

When she arrived, they placed a computer chip in her brain to monitor activity, and it had changed her. She cried in her sleep and sometimes had outbursts during the day. Removing the chip was unsafe years ago, but with the serum, now there was a possibility of safe removal. Sven tried to imagine Julia outside, but it was a definite stretch of the imagination.

"Has she been getting her regular doses of the serum?" asked Sven.

"They are now spaced apart, considering the lack of quantity, but she is still improving."

Sven hooked Adam by the crook of the arm, forcing him to turn around and look at him. "What is wrong? Why can't you look at me? Is there something you want to say to me?"

"Look, Sven, I'm just worried about you, okay? But I don't want to be all preachy to you, either."

"Say what you need to say. I am a big boy. I can handle it." Another scientist walked by them, giving Sven a second look, and then scurried away. "What's the latest rumor, Adam? Why don't you fill me in?"

"It's not the rumors I am worried about." Adam scanned Sven from head to toe in a disapproving look.

"Why don't we walk and talk? We still have a lot to do today." They proceeded their path.

"You look pretty torn up," he said. "I talked to Jesse."

"I figured," Sven replied, curious about what he had told him.

"Something about him going over to your house and your smashed car, and you were on the property over by the tree? Why would you go there by yourself? That could have been dangerous." Adam stopped himself, putting his hands in front of him. "By the looks of you, it was dangerous, if that's what happened. I don't believe everything I hear. You look like...heck."

"I got in a fight with a mutant, if you need to know, and that's why I look like heck." Sven motioned him to an empty room, and shut the door. He didn't want the whole hospital to hear what he was talking about, so he motioned him to an empty room where the cameras weren't monitored regularly due to the absence of a patient. "Yes, I went to the property that Charles Williams purchased. It's wrong what he is doing. Did you know he didn't buy the property where the tree of life is, but someone fudged the paperwork? I took care of it, but wanted to make sure that Charles was sticking to his side of the property." Sven purposely left out the destruction that he accomplished.

"And where does this mutant fit in with all of this? Does Charles have a pet mutant?" Adam scoffed.

"No, a dog." When Adam gave him a strange look, he continued. "The mutant came out of the woods when I was there, and I didn't have any protection with me. I was busy."

"I can imagine." Adam squinted his eyes together. "What did you do?"

"I rushed into the car, and that's why it looked like a wreck. Look, my car had the tranquilizer gun, and now I'm safe."

Adam rubbed his chin. "So, what's your next move?"

"I don't know what you're talking about." Sven thought about what Charles said about saving Hannah. He had to figure this out, which way he was going to go. If Charles found out what he was doing, there was no working with the man. "There is no next move. As far as I go, I am done. What happens, happens, and there is nothing I can do about it."

Sven wished he was around a live camera right now, and Charles could hear what he was saying. He would know Sven was serious about keeping his end of the bargain, even though he wasn't.

"Doesn't sound like you." They left the room and continued down the hall. "Why the secrecy?"

"If someone finds out what I did, it's against the law. I got into enough trouble last year. I don't want to make a habit of it." Sven hated lying to him. That wasn't why. Sven bit his bottom lip and hoped Adam couldn't see through him.

"Do any of us?" They reached Julia's room, and both sanitized their hands. Julia was curled up against her headboard, head between her knees, her eyes closed. Anyone else would think she was sleeping, but the scientists knew better.

"What's going on in that head of yours?" asked Sven, and Julia jumped, returning to reality. He wondered if Julia could creep into people's minds and see what he was considering working with Charles to bring Hannah back. Wanting to make sure he was true to his word about working on something to bring her back, a trip to his pharmaceutical company was in order. He wasn't about to wait for Charles to get around to making a meeting. Time was of the essence.

When Julia wanted to escape mentally from boredom, she would close her eyes and imagine another world by making up stories in her head to entertain herself.

"A mystery where the golden treasure was in danger, and the noble prince to find it and protect it." She smiled.

"What do you want to be when you grow up?" asked Adam. "Someday you would make a great movie producer."

She laughed at him. "Movie producer? I am going to write books, the best you have ever read." Her face wrinkled in pain, and she hissed through her teeth. Her eyes glowed brighter than ever, and tears fell down her cheeks. Both of the scientists ran to her, one on each side of her.

"We're here," reassured Adam.

"You're going to be okay," said Sven, and after Adam nodded to him, Sven rushed to the cabinet, pressed his fingerprint on the scanner, and opened it. Riffling through the contents of the top drawer, he loaded up a spidomed and attached it to her arm. The medication calmed her, the spidomed dispersing the sedative and pain medication at the fastest way possible.

"Thank you," she muttered, leaning against the headboard, slack, sweat pouring down her forehead. "I love you."

Julia fell asleep.

Sven and Adam put the covers over her, making sure she was comfortable. Sven moved her pillow right underneath her head. He made notes in her chart, and after checking all her vitals with a simple scan across the forehead, loaded up the information.

Closing the door behind them, Adam said, "she's going to need some more serum. We're going to have to figure something out."

"We will," said Sven. "Do you think you could help me with something?"

"Anything, my friend. How can I help?"

"And Jesse, too." Sven remembered his promise with Jesse after he cut the lines from the cameras Jesse was spying on. "I promised we would work as a team and I don't plan on backing out." *Except for the deal with Charles. That's my little secret.*

"I believe he's at the end of the hall." Adam motioned him to follow with a flick of the wrist and a smile just in time for Jesse to open a door, speed through, and shut it. Out of breath, he leaned against the wall and tilted his head back, closing his eyes.

"Jesse?" asked Sven.

"I'm fine." He raised his index finger. "Just one minute." Sven could hear growling from the other side of the door before total silence from the room. "Whew, those medications must have finally kicked in. The serum is, well, kind of working."

"That's what I wanted to talk to you two about," said Sven, leading them away from the public hallway and into his office. Adam was the last to come in, shutting the door behind him. "I am still worried about Charles and what he is doing with the tree, and I think we should do some digging. We need to get into that facility."

Jesse leaned against the wall while Sven sat in a chair, turning to face him.

"Do you think that's the best way?" Adam looked skeptical. "That man has a lot of money and tons of security. He owns a security company, for crying out loud."

"That's why we have to all work together," said Sven. "I can't do this alone. I'm going to need your help for the future of this world."

Jesse smiled with a smirk. "I could slide right in and out of that place and blend in like a chameleon." He straightened his collar. "I am so glad you agreed we would work together on this."

"Yes, together, Jesse. You're not going to do this on your own," said Sven.

Adam rubbed his chin. "It might not be so hard to do with careful planning."

"I'm in," said Jesse. "All right guys, I have hacked into his cameras in the woods. I'm sure I can somehow get into his facility's cameras."

"And you're definitely going to need a disguise," said Adam. "We all are. Most of the people in this town know who we are, and someone is going to spot us."

"Let's get to work," said Sven.

# CHAPTER SEVENTEEN

"Be careful," Charles warned as one of his associates reached for the tree frog at the tree of life, the frog almost slipping from his hands. He grasped it, placing it in a container with air holes.

The sun glistened off the leaves, the recent rain leaving moisture on them and giving them a shine. Charles looked up through the branches and thin metal bars, a ray of sunlight shining through reflecting off the metal, and wondered what it was like for Adam Davidson to find the first tree frog after what they thought was total extinction, not even sure what he may have found. And now it's mine, along with all the power of life and death. I will go down in the history books.

Placing his hand on the bark, he remembered when he was a boy and didn't understand the dangers of the world. Sneaking out of the house, he played in the woods until found, grounded for weeks. Fortunate enough to be discovered by his father before a mutant, he was unharmed. But for that short time playing outside, he had never felt so free.

If only the world was different.

Shaking off his thoughts, he rolled his eyes at himself. *It's not my responsibility to fix the damn world. I have bigger things to worry about.*

He assigned three of the scientists on his appointed team to gather the tree frogs. Around the perimeter of the tree, he had also hired five MCS to keep them all safe and gave them a bonus for unexpected guests. "No government official will tell me what I can and can't do. Damn state." Five tall, burly men in tactical gear with paralyzer and tranquilizer guns at the ready kept their eyes on the rest of the forest, not paying attention so much to the scientists. Focused, they had a job to do.

Charles stepped out of the dome to give them more room to work and gather the frogs.

*Now he will leave me alone, thought Charles. Now there is something I have that he wants. It's always good to have a backup plan, just in case he doesn't take the bait.* The thought made him smile, a slight chuckle escaping. *I have him right where I want him.*

"Mr. Williams, how many should we gather?" asked one of the men, trying to get his grip around another frog.

"As many as possible," he replied, thinking *it is going to take a lot of serum to accomplish what he set out to do.* One of the MCS leapt near Charles in an effort to protect him, his tranquilizer gun at the ready.

"Over there!" he shouted to the other men. Growling came from the nearby bushes, and out flew a bat-like creature, the wings of a bat but a green, scaly body and an ape-like face in structure. Its wingspan was five feet, its body the size of a toddler.

And it flew fast.

The MCS man, Mike, shot at it and missed the first time, the mutant flying over them and continuing through the trees.

"Let's hurry," said Charles. "Make sure to do your job," he snapped at Mike.

Mike gave him the you've-got-to-be-kidding-me look for one second, returning his focus to the sky.

The bat returned, its webbed feet grazing the top of the tree, leaves falling as they were hit.

"Okay, let's grab the frogs and get out of here," said Charles.

"I got this," said one of the other MCS guys, David, a younger man with a boyish face. His arms were bigger than the rest of his body, bulging through the gear. The tranquilizer gun struck the mutant, while his flying slowed and he dropped from the sky.

Charles felt warmth from something running through his hair. The smell.

"Could you have shot him before he shit all over me?" Grabbing a handkerchief from his pocket, he wiped some of the feces from his hair. "I'm done for the day. Let's get these back to the lab."

— • —

# CHAPTER EIGHTEEN

*Before I consider anything, we need to check out what Charles has first. I am not waiting for him to give the information to me. What if it's not accurate? Thank God I'm a doctor and would know. I wouldn't put it past him swindling someone. Julia needs the serum, Hannah might need the serum...I need to make sure there is plenty to go around. With help from my friends, we have a better chance to pull this off. We have to.*

Grabbing the press badge Adam stole from a real live reporter, Sven took another look at the picture and held it up to him in front of the mirror. Cutting out the old picture, one of Sven was in his place. The reporter was waiting outside of Juniper Ridge to get an interview on the progression of the serum effectiveness and the rate of the new patients, right before Adam told him to get lost. Lou Smith yanked his press I.D. in Adam's face. Adam grasped it, pointed down the road, and told him to get the hell off the property.

Lucky for this plan, Lou had never gotten it back.

Placing it around his neck, he grabbed a device that acted as both a camera and recording implement that looked like a pencil. All the reporters these days had them. Sven liked the nostalgic look. Slicking his hair back, he thought of everything they had done in the last two days. He hoped all the appointments and information added online worked.

Time is everything.

Sven grumbled as he tried to stretch in the tiny car he borrowed from his neighbor. It was best to travel in something else to be undetected, at least at first. The traffic was heavy for six in the morning on a Saturday. No matter. He knew Charles' pharmaceutical company ran twenty-four hours, seven days a week.

The monumental building didn't intimidate him, but made him feel more comfortable. With such a vast campus, he could blend in with the crowd. The gate opened as someone swiped their badge. Sven snuck in behind him right before the gate shut, surprised Charles didn't have better security than a simple swipe card.

Of course, he wasn't in the building yet.

Usually aware of his surroundings because of mutants, he was good at keeping aware. This was different. He didn't want to be recognized by Charles or any of his workers. Who knew if he spread the word of what Sven got away with? Would he want to be known as someone that was taken advantage of? Sven doubted it.

Sven had a knit hat on, dark blue, that was pulled down directly over his eyes. Deciding trying too hard to look inconspicuous was having the opposite effect, he threw the hat in the back seat, forgetting that he slicked his hair back and now it flew in all directions. He fidgeted with his glasses. His puffy jacket made him appear twice in size, and underneath he wore simple blue jeans and a sweater. Black glasses with thick rims replaced Sven's small spectacles that matched the picture in his fake I.D. Same prescription, just the ones that he had years ago. Straightening his coat, he slammed his door and waited for the tiny vehicle to crumble.

Showtime.

The entrance was massive, and Sven's eyes grew wide as he pulled on the door with no luck. He stepped back and fiddled with his jacket as if he wasn't ready to go in and really knew how to get in the building, watching the people enter. Fingerprint scan, click from the door with a green light, and access granted. They had to have a way for visitors to enter, he reasoned. Sven scratched the inside of his ear, brushing the microscopic transmitter placed there.

Jesse's voice echoed in his ear, and Sven jumped. "Security cameras are running on a loop. Your appointment is on the computer, Sven. I can feel your tension from here. Relax your shoulders and try to look like you fit in." Knowing Jesse was hiding in the shrubbery watching him, Sven took a deep breath and loosened up.

"Do you need help, Sir?" asked an employee dressed in a three-piece suit. Not a hair out of place, a wrinkle in his wardrobe, and his smile was just too perfect. While Sven usually admired these things, this time it creeped him out.

Sven returned the smile. "Oh, if you wouldn't mind. I'm with the newspaper and I have an appointment today..." Sven pressed his index finger to the fingerprint scan. "It's not working."

"Someone should be out here to escort you in. I can, but you have to stay with me until at least the front desk."

"Oh, thank you," Sven stammered, using his nervousness to his advantage. "This building is much bigger than the newsroom. It's intimidating."

"It's not as scary as it looks. I'm Hunter. Follow me." Hunter pressed his finger to the scanner and led Sven inside. "And you are?"

"Lou, and thank you so much, Hunter." They entered a room with hundreds of people in and out, groups talking in the lobby, the building buzzing with activity. It's as if no one in the building knew of the devastation happening right outside these walls. A U-shaped granite countertop lined with computers and receptionists planted in the center of all the action, greeting people as they walked in the door.

"Hello," Sven said to the available one, Hunter close on his heels.

She gave him her pristine smile. Christine was the name on her tag, and answered, "what can I do for you, sir? Do you have an appointment?"

"He works for the local newspaper," said Hunter. "Good luck." After shooting Sven a smile, he disappeared down the hall.

Literally disappeared. Sven wondered how many teleportation machines Charles had set up.

His attention moved back to the front desk. Tapping his badge, he said, "I'm Lou Smith. I made an appointment on-line."

"Just let me check his schedule." She punched some buttons on the computer and looked through the day, then looked again. "I don't know how this happened. The computer never makes this mistake. It appears that someone placed an appointment where there wasn't an available slot. I'm so sorry. It looks like you're going to have to reschedule."

"I understand." He hung his head. "Well, could I just talk to some of his associates if they aren't too busy? Anyone here that works with him that is available?" Avoiding him at all costs. I can't believe that computer trick worked. Thank you, Jesse.

"Let me see." The glow from the computer reflected in her eyes as she muttered names to herself so quietly Sven couldn't understand. He put his elbow on the edge of the counter and leaned in. "I'm sorry, Mr. Smith. They are all too busy."

"I understand." Sven hung his head, fiddling with his recorder/camera pencil. "It's okay. It's just I don't know when I will be able to come back."

"Why is that?" Her eyes cast downward, concern laced her voice. "Is everything okay with you?"

"I am about ready to retire, and this is my last big story. I know how long it takes to get an appointment here, and I just don't think it will happen in time. But..." He let out a long sigh, "it's not your fault. It's okay."

Turning on his heel, he took his time toward the entrance, when he heard her sweet voice yell over the crowd of people.

"Mr. Smith! Mr. Smith!" His face brightened as he returned to the counter. "You could go down to the labs, but you will need a special pass, something to go with the one you're wearing." Clicking again on the computer, she handed him a ready-made badge that read Panacea Daily with the Williams Pharmaceutical logo in the corner. "I wish you all the best."

"Christine," he said, glancing at her badge, "you can call me Lou."

"Okay, Lou. You are good to go." Her toothy grin dropped into a line as her eyes narrowed, and Sven's heart stopped. She shook her finger at him. "Lou Smith. I thought your name sounded familiar. You wrote that piece about the additional steps of what we can do to help the environment. That was a great article." Her smile returned.

Sven let out a pent up breath. "Thanks. If more people did those things, we would all be a lot better off."

"Let me show you where you need to go." Putting a closed sign at her station, she waved him to follow her. He held in a chuckle when she stood. With her green silk blouse and black pencil skirt that went just below her knee, she wore black sneakers. Smart. No one would see them with her sitting at the counter.

"Nice shoes," he commented.

"I like being comfortable," she said, taking note of his smile. "You're going to like Steve. He has worked here for over twenty years." The reception branched off into four directions, each hallway a sign above it to indicate where they led to. They read, "Business Offices", "Distribution", "Manufacture", and "Labs". The halls were wide enough he could walk next to her without crowding her. "How long have you worked for the paper?"

"Time flies so fast. Must have been twenty-five years by now." The walls were a pale green with pictures of beaches and trees. "And where is Mr. Williams's office?"

"On the top floor. A special elevator with only his access goes up there, but like I said, he's not here."

*Special access. I wonder if I could find anything...*

"Of course, I was just curious. It comes with the job."

The lab was full of men and women in white lab coats, working around machines and typing on computers. The walls were white as well, all the equipment flawlessly clean. Sven felt right at home. From the corner of his eye, he spotted a familiar face in a white lab coat, Adam. Sven was careful that his eyes didn't linger too long. The man next to the front desk introduced himself to Sven and gave a questioning look at Christine.

"He's doing an article in the paper about Mr. Williams. Charles is always saying that we could use all the positive publicity that we can get."

"I'm not here for publicity, but I guess I have some time." He looked down at Sven. "Steve Gardner," he said.

There was something instantly that Sven liked about Steve, and he almost introduced himself as Sven, but stopped himself. "Nice to meet you."

"Well, if you two are okay, I have other work to do," said Christine, leaving the two by themselves.

"I could give you a tour, but there are certain areas that are off-limits to visitors."

"Whatever you can tell me. I'm sure this article would be very interesting to the general public. Is it okay if I turn on my recorder?" Steve nodded and Sven flicked the switch on his "pencil". The first machine tested blood samples. Steve explained they did this with new medications after people that volunteered to try it, to see if their medical condition they were trying to treat had improved. They also had notes they went through about the condition and the patients.

"What's he like?" asked Sven. "As a boss?"

"Who?"

"Charles Williams. The man behind the title. Billionaire extraordinaire." Sven extended his hands in a grand gesture. He leaned forward and craned his head out. "Seriously, what is he really like?"

"Well…" Steve paused. "He's a great boss. He works all the time. It's like he's trying to save the world or something." Sven fought off a grunt. *Save the world, my ass.* Something about the way Steve talked. It was like he was speaking off of a reader board.

"Really? Off the record." Sven held up his hands, turning the recorder off. "I'm just curious."

"Check this out." Steve leaned over the computer, punching in buttons at rapid speed until a file came up. Amputees listed with data of a drug that could improve the chance of an appendage adapting to the patient so he or she could have an actual arm or leg function donated by another.

Sven leaned down to read the information. *This wouldn't work. The connection of the nerves and muscle structure would be virtually impossible.* He had to keep his opinions to himself. Just a reporter and nothing more. "Who knows about this?" said Sven.

"Just the people that work at this lab, and not even everyone here."

"I don't understand. Then why are you showing this to me?"

"I know what some people think of my boss, but he isn't all bad. I wouldn't put this specific data in your article because we haven't achieved success yet, but just to keep in mind, he is trying to help people. Maybe that would help you with the article."

"What makes you think he will succeed?"

"He has created enough drugs to make a multitude of cash. He has even created something to help with the mutants. I know he's been working with the serum to learn how to develop more. I'm not an idiot. I know there's a shortage. So it isn't a cure, but it is something that helps with the symptoms. And he created something for the addicts. His family may have had money when he was growing up, but booted out at eighteen, he had to build his own life. And with it, he built his empire. So you can put that in your article."

"What else can you tell me about him?" Sven heard something in the background, but he couldn't tell where it was coming from. There was room in the back of the laboratory, no windows, and locked with a keypad. Just a shell of white.

"What's in the room?" asked Sven.

"What room?" *Oh, he's playing dumb.*

Sven pointed to the locked room in the back. "That's the room I'm asking about. Don't be coy."

"Supply closet. It's almost time for my break. Do you want to get a coffee?" Steve began walking toward the door, motioning with a sideways bob of the head for Sven to follow.

"Including doughnuts?"

"Sure." Steve shrugged.

"What's in there first?" Sven pointed to the mysterious room.

"I'll explain it all to you when we get something to eat. I can't think when I'm hungry."

"That makes two of us. I'm there." Steve stopped to talk to another man, checking data on a monster of a machine close to the secret room. "And show the new guy the machine. I'm going on a break. You're in charge."

Sven looked over to see an older gentleman going into the supply closet. 1975043. Enter. 1229756. He prayed that Adam, otherwise known as the "new guy", was looking, too, but didn't want to be obvious. Sven repeated these three times in his mind, praying he could remember them. Sven followed him to a cafeteria with one wall of hot food and a corner with desserts. Drinks were in the middle, hot coffee, hot chocolate, and soda. Steve and Sven found a table in the corner away from people, although for the massive space, there weren't that many.

Sven dug into his maple bar, savoring the sweetness as it tickled his tongue. The hot coffee, strong and bitter, balanced it all out. He closed his eyes and moaned.

"You really love your doughnuts," said Steve, chuckling.

"I haven't had a maple bar in I don't know how long." After another sip of his coffee, he cleared his throat. "I want information about Charles. I'm curious. What do you know about him? What motivates him to build all this?" He opened his arms. This would have been a better question in the lab, but he was sure Steve knew what he meant.

Steve looked around and said under his breath, "You haven't figured all that out yet? Greed. The man likes money, and he likes power. No one tells Charles what to do."

Sven noted the lack of cameras in the cafeteria and assumed that's what was bringing out the honesty. "Well, I figured out that much. What about his family? His parents? Does he have a wife? It seems the whole world knows him, but they don't really KNOW him."

"He's a very private man. I've been working here a long time, and that's the only reason I know what I know. He was married a long time ago, but his wife left him. I think it's because he spent his entire life working. But what do I know?"

"People get divorced for all kinds of reasons." Sven shrugged. "There might have been something going on that no one knew about. No kids?" Sven thought of Hannah, and he grew somber. He remembered the crash, the shattering of glass echoed in his mind for one brief second, yelling for Lucas, and was gone again.

"They had a daughter, Kimberly. I thought that he had custody, but I don't know what happened to her. I assumed that his wife took her, because I never hear him talking about Kimberly anymore. Strange...I think she was the only one that brought out the goodness in him."

*And I thought it was only his dog.*

"I don't know much about his personal life. He's usually here, or at his teleportation company. All about innovation with him. He treats his employees well, and that's why we stay." Steve munched on his cinnamon roll. "I hope that's enough for your story."

"I think that will do it for today. I will find my way out." Skipping out on the information about the secret room. Sven had a feeling to not push it. Easy going was the way for his disguise. But wouldn't a good reporter ask? Inconspicuous was more important.

"You're my responsibility. Besides, you might get lost in this place. I'll walk you out. You don't want to finish your dessert?"

"That's what's great about doughnuts. They're easy to eat while traveling." Sven took another bite, swigging the rest of the coffee, almost burning his mouth. It was time to leave. He had a bad feeling that Charles could show up at any time or that any one of them would be recognized.

"And everything that we talked about, could we keep it between us? I don't want anyone to see it until it shows up in the paper."

"Sure." Steve gave him a nod before walking him out, back to the front doors. Sven felt like everyone had their eyes on him as he traveled. Did he have an invisible sign on his back that read, "I'm going against Charles Williams. Anyone want to join me?" Some looks held curiosity, some admiration. Maybe some of them knew who he really was? If they did, they weren't correcting anyone.

Thank God.

He hoped he was just being paranoid.

He wondered about the room in the back of the lab, and knowing that Steve returned to the cafeteria to finish his cinnamon roll, looked around to see if anyone was paying attention, and headed back in the lab's direction. There was a hall closet with the door ajar, revealing a white lab coat that was hanging up. In an effort to blend in even more, he took off his jacket, tossing it in the closet, and slipped on the lab coat. The coat hung past his knees and the sleeves reached the middle of his palms. *Well, being too big is better than too small.* Everyone was focusing on their own thing, and didn't notice the change. Perhaps they thought he was just an employee changing. His badge from a distance could be mistaken for an employee one.

He was glad Christine was busy helping someone else and hadn't noticed him backtracking.

Don't look like you are up to something, he told himself, casually entering the lab. He looked down and made his way to the locked room. At least with the lab coat, he blended in better and looked like he belonged. Even though it was too large, the lab coat made him feel more himself.

"Can I help you?" asked a woman, tall and thin with pink tourmaline earrings. He blinked twice and she was not so thin, her earrings gone. His mind was playing tricks on him. The young woman wasn't Jill, her smile told him.

"I'm new here." He tucked his badge partway into the lab coat and hoped she didn't see him walking around with Steve, but she didn't look familiar. "It will just take me a moment to remember the combination. I'm good."

She distanced herself, but he knew she was still watching him. 19750...oh, what was next? He guessed thirty-four. After hitting enter, the red light illuminated. Wrong number. Glancing up, he saw the earlier woman tilt her head.

Sven closed his eyes, took a deep breath, and took his time. 1975043. Yes, green! Just one more set of numbers. 1229756. The light glowed green, and he slipped into the room, shutting the door behind him. Out of the corner of his eye, he spotted Adam investigating the machine that he was supposed to be learning only a few feet from where Sven slipped through the door.

The lack of windows was helpful, and the security cameras were on, but he knew it was still running in a loop for a couple more hours. They blinked red, as they weren't working properly. Thankful for his disguise, he took in the room at a glance. He wasn't sure what he was going to expect when he opened the door, but it wasn't this.

A simple room, it had a file cabinet, a computer, and a chair. Sitting in the chair, he opened the file cabinet, convinced he wouldn't be able to get into the computer. Opening the file cabinet, it glowed a bright red, and an alarm sounded.

He slammed it shut, hiding underneath the desk, closing his eyes and waiting for someone to show up. Maybe they wouldn't see him. Where else was he supposed to go? He should have figured it would have an alarm on it. He gripped the spidomed that he brought for emergencies, mutant or medical break in, and stayed quiet.

The noise was ear-splitting. He heard commotion right outside and all the scientists moving out of their chairs. The door flew open, and Sven's heart stopped. Trying to see from underneath the desk, he just saw someone wearing black pants. Throwing the spidomed, he caught a part of his leg, enough of the tranquilizer to stun him, but not much more.

"What the hell?" The guard leaned over and grabbed Sven by the collar. "What are you doing here?"

Sven leaned behind him to grab the spidomed and position it properly, but he was holding him too far away. "Research." Sven flew open the drawer once more on the file cabinet with his foot, and the alarm was disabled by this time. It did provide enough of a distraction for the guard to move his head, and after loosening his grip Sven reached farther, planting the spidomed on his back.

The guard quickly let go of Sven, the guard passing out in a heap on the floor.

He had minutes, he guessed. Sven grabbed papers and shoved them underneath his lab coat.

Running out of the room, he ran through the lab with everyone staring behind him, dropping the papers underneath the machine that Adam was working on. No one seemed to notice with the rattling of chairs and lab instruments falling off the tables as he moved through the room.

"Hey, there he is!" He heard someone yell behind him. Sven didn't look, but broke out in a sprint, men behind him. He weaved through people, knocking them over, pushing them down, until he saw the doors. More men were after him. He could hear their feet behind him. "Someone stop him!"

Sven felt something wiz past his head. Whatever they were shooting at him, if it was a gun, this wasn't worth dying over. He stopped and held up his hands.

"Don't move." A tall, burly man in a leather jacket grabbed onto Sven's wrists, hooking them together. "You are in so much trouble." He jerked him away from the lobby. "Show is over. Everyone get back to work." People murmured to each other as they headed back to their desks or workplaces.

"I can explain."

"Oh, and you will explain," said the guard, Mason printed on his shirt underneath his jacket, peeking out.

The guard took him to a room adjacent to the larger room that read security above it. Mason slammed the door behind him, locking it and told Sven to sit. The room was almost totally dark, with only two chairs. Sven frantically tried to think of some fabrication that he could come up with. Why would someone break into the room, and he noticed the size of Mason, hoping his heart was as big as his arms. There had to be a soft spot with this guy.

"I wanted information about the new drug that the company has been working on, for the mutants," said Sven.

Mason crossed his arms and looked at Sven like a lower life form.

Sven squirmed in his seat. "I need it."

Mason harrumphed. "Why? You aren't a mutant, are you?" He leaned in and squinted his eyes at Sven, as if examining him.

"No, but my brother. I love him very much, and you know how hard it is to get the serum right now. He had a reaction. He is very ill, and I just thought that if he could have the new serum, something better with less side effects, it might make him okay." His wrists sore from the restraints, it wasn't so hard for a tear to roll down his cheek. "I promised his wife that I would try."

"You can tell it all to the police," said Mason. "I don't care about your sob story."

"But it's not a story, it's the truth." Sven straightened his back and fought the urge to bite his bottom lip. *This was not the way this was supposed to happen. What is Charles going to do with me now? What is going to happen with me already having a record? It's small, but I still broke the law in the past.*

"What did you find?" asked Mason.

Sven looked down at the ground. "Nothing. Just a locked file cabinet, but no medicine whatsoever." He fought to stop the shakiness of his voice. His stomach twisted in knots and he felt like vomiting.

"Where is your brother? I would assume he is at Juniper Ridge since he is undergoing treatment for his mutation condition." Sven tilted his head and shrugged, indicating a yes. *I know I look unsure. He is going to get me arrested. I am screwing this up.* Sven leaned down to pretend to tie his shoe, and tugged at his fake I.D., slipping it in his pocket. This fake identity won't be helping him at all right now.

Sven merely nodded for an answer. *Where was Adam? Jesse was supposed to be somewhere on the grounds as a repairman. Adam better have that paperwork I dropped, or all this is for nothing.*

"I will give them a call." Mason was on the phone with Juniper Ridge for ten minutes, going through the main desk, finding the correct department, and answering a number of questions. Sven was so still, his muscles stiffened from lack of movement. His tight shoulders filled with pain from his wrists hooked together behind him. Leaning forward to try and get more comfortable, he listened attentively to everything that he was saying, although he couldn't hear much. *Who was Mason talking to? They wouldn't even know what I was up to. I am in so much trouble. We should have thought all of this out better.*

Mason thanked them, then hung up the phone right before shoving it in his pocket. Moving across the room, his gaze steady on Sven before he struck a button by the door.

The doors made a powerful latching noise and Mason smiled at Sven.

Sven swallowed a lump in his throat.

"This company will not tolerate break-ins, snoops, or spies. Or liars for that matter. Juniper Ridge has never heard of you, Lou, if that even is your real name." Sven said nothing. "It doesn't matter to me. Let's see how you do with some time in jail." Mason laughed at him. "I'm not going to hurt you. I'm just keeping you in my sight so you don't get away."

Sven sat without saying a word, trying to avoid the gaze Mason had on him, who leaned back in his chair without speaking. Sven liked it better when the man was talking, and he tried to envision what he was thinking. Did he have some plan for him other than jail?

The door lock releases clicked and two officers entered the room. Sven recognized them immediately with all the break-ins at Juniper Ridge with the serum. He stared at the floor, now avoiding everyone's eyes in the room, wishing he could melt into the wall and disappear. *If only I could teleport just thinking about it.*

"You're under arrest for breaking and entering," said Anderson. "Do you have anything to say for yourself?"

"No sir," Sven muttered.

"Stand up and look at me."

Sven stood. *Please don't remember me and have the disguise do its job.* Their eyes locked, followed by a long pause.

"You look familiar," he said. "We'll sort it out at the station."

The other officer read him his rights. With Sven agreeing to go peacefully, the three of them entered the hall. Everyone they passed watched him, and he heard some murmurs that he tried to ignore. Reaching the front desk, Christina stopped her data entry, frowned and shook her head. *Yes, you helped me and I'm a fraud.* He couldn't meet her gaze and looking the opposite way, spotted Adam in the corner of his eye.

And he couldn't help noticing Adam holding a stack of papers in his arms.

— · —

# CHAPTER NINETEEN

As they shoved Sven in the back of the police car, when the men were talking in the front seat, Sven could hear his pea-size transmitter in his ear.

"Damn thing quit working." Jesse's voice relaxed him, no matter what he was saying. "I couldn't hear anything once you entered the building. Hang tight and we'll bail you out."

"You better hurry," Sven muttered.

The officers grew quiet up front, and the passenger leaned back. "What was that?"

"Nothing."

Instead of looking out the window, Sven slouched down in an effort to be more out of sight. He went through everything he did and said from the moment he entered the facility in his mind. If he waited to go into the room, he might not have gotten caught, but then again, the opportunity might have been gone forever.

The rain left designs on the windows as he peered out from his slouched position and he sat up straighter, figuring through the rain and darkness of the gloomy day, who was going to see him anyway? The clouds continued to roll in.

They stopped on the side of the police station, pulled into the protective room, and the thunk of the metal door behind them echoed. This was a mutant safety step a lot like what everyone had in their garages at home.

In the first room, a thorough search for anything he might have stolen or anything against the law took place. They asked him what his name was. There was no use lying to them now; he would need his true identity to get out of this mess.

"Sven Olander."

Both officers pulled back for a second, and the arresting one broke the silence. "From Juniper Ridge? I knew you looked familiar." The officer's stern face relaxed.

"You understand, Dr. Olander, we still have a job to do," said the other, who found the recorder tucked in his ear. "And what is this?"

Sven was about ready to say a hearing aid. He was older than them and it resembled an old-fashioned one, but he didn't want to get into any more trouble. They also took his "pencil" recorder.

"I communicate with people. Sometimes I forget to put my phone watch on in the morning." He flashed his wrist. "Like this morning, see?"

They removed both devices and kept them.

Thrown into a cell five feet square, the door slammed shut. No windows, just cement walls and a layer of dust blanketed the room. So tired, but he didn't dare lean on any of the walls or sit on the floor. He wasn't even certain he could get back up. What was Adam doing right now? Did he get out of the facility with the papers? Were the cops talking to Jesse over the earpiece or was Jesse listening in to everything that was going on?

His legs feeling wobbly, they slip and he sat on the hard floor of the prison cell. A moldy smell hung in the air and penetrated his nostrils. Coughing, it made its way down his throat.

"While the whole world has gotten more modern, jails are worse," said Sven to himself.

All that was in the cell was a toilet and a sink, which he could only see the silhouette in the darkened cell. With the combination of the stench and anxiety, nausea hit him. From where he was sitting, if he vomited it was a simple pivot away. Taking deep breaths, he was okay.

*Focus on something else. Next plan of attack: find out what is in that paperwork. Gather with Jesse and Adam to figure out the next step.* All the while, he had to be careful. Charles did have something he wanted, and more than that, he was buddies with the owner holding Hannah's body.

Closing his eyes, he remembered the time he visited her after they took her from their home. The hum of the machine stopped, the glow of the chamber dimmed, and his dear wife was unsalvageable, never to return to him. My imagination. Everything is fine.

"Okay, Olander, someone is here to bail you out," he heard from the hallway. Yawning and rubbing his eyes, he concluded he must have dozed off from all the excitement of the day.

Standing up, he wiped the dust off his clothes and followed the jailer down the hall to the front of the building. A new face to him, the man was young enough to be a cadet. With a straight back and stiff form, Sven wondered if he was trying to look professional, tough, or if he was nervous. Perhaps all three. Sven said nothing until he saw Adam's face and was instantly relieved.

"They dropped all the charges, so you're lucky. The owner of Williams must be pretty understanding."

Adam handed the lady at the front desk his credit card. "Are you ready?" he asked Sven. Expressionless. Not mad, frustrated, nothing.

They made it out to Adam's truck and Adam was quiet until they had the doors closed and locked.

Adam exhaled.

"I wanted to do something, but what could I do? It would have blown my cover in a second. Watching them take you away..."

"Did Jesse make it out all right?" asked Sven.

"Behind you," replied Adam, and Sven spotted Jesse's jeep in the rear-view mirror. The relief calmed him. "He'll just follow us. Are you hungry? I could get you something to eat."

"Just tell me," said Sven, "did you get the papers I dropped? There's something in all that paperwork."

Adam paused, then smiled, lifting up a stack of papers. Raising his eyebrows, he said, "And I have more."

"More? What else did you find?"

Adam pulled out into the parking lot, jumping on the highway and navigating through the traffic.

*Why does he do this to me?* "You have the papers, so what else did you find?"

"A vial of serum from his company. Only half an ounce - the vial is an off-yellow hue, black top, and a red line down one side." Adam made a turn into the main part of town toward Sven's house. "Sound familiar?"

Sven remembered the last addict that was admitted and the vial they had found on her - it fit the exact description.

"Could have stolen it from Charles' company," Sven said, "or something else."

"I'm betting on something else." Adam's expression was like a kid on Christmas morning. "We did tests on the traces of serum the patient had on her. The DNA was such a small fraction, laced with other drugs."

"Head to my house," said Sven. "We have to talk and it's private there."

"You got it," agreed Adam, heading to the east side of town. The roads were busy on a Saturday night. Sven stared out the window, lost in thought.

*Does Charles know I have the vial that could land him in jail or at least ruin his reputation be the reason why he dropped the charges? Or is it because I may be the only one that can help him?*

— · —

# Chapter Twenty

Sven opened the garage door the next morning to head to the grocery store. Saturday night, after Adam and Jesse arrived at the house, they agreed they would split up the tasks. Jesse and Adam took the vial back to the lab to analyze on Sunday while Sven could take the paperwork, reading through the stack to see what he could find. He only had time to get half-way through them, making notes in the margins. He had a hard time believing what he was reading. The man was getting close, but Sven could see Charles and his associates had little knowledge of the serum and mutants. Not the history like he had. Ideas scribbled in Sven's handwriting with a bold blue pen covered the bare spots entirely.

Sven's stomach began growling, and there was no way he could focus on an empty stomach. Black circles rimmed his eyes, his face an ashen hue. Every time he closed his eyes to rest them from the small print, he saw the tight jail cell, the smell and the filth foremost in his mind. He patted the briefcase next to him full of documents, not about ready to let them leave his side.

Stopping abruptly at the limo parked behind him, his heart sped up and pulse raced. He could barely put it into park. *Why would Charles come after him now? Captured to be tortured so he wouldn't share secrets? Beaten to death?* He went to pull back into the garage and close the door, but a man was getting out of the car faster than Sven could move.

"No need to be alarmed," said the man, holding up his hands as if in surrender. "Mr. Williams would like to speak with you. I suggest you get in the car, sir." His eyes darted around. "There is no protection from mutants out here."

"I can't drive my own car to his residence? I know where he lives."

The driver raised his eyebrows and shook his head, as three others got out of the car, twice the size of the driver. They towered over Sven, their hands folded in front of them, their feet planted on the ground far apart, and stared straight at him.

"And bring the paperwork."

Sven was about ready to say *what paperwork?* But decided against it, considering it was sitting in the passenger seat. The biggest man started toward Sven, and Sven held up his hands.

*The notes. He will have all of them.*

"Okay, just let me grab it." Opening the car door, he gripped the handle of the briefcase, picturing slamming the heavy item into someone's face, but four against one were bad odds. *He hasn't done anything to me yet,* and Sven couldn't help but wonder why. *Was there something Sven had that Charles need-*

ed? Surely he had back-ups to the papers, but he didn't want them in Sven's possession. *I thought he wanted my help?*

Sven closed the garage with the car small enough to clear the door. Wouldn't want to come home to any mutants lurking. Even with the spacious limo, Sven sat in between two of the men as told, legs and arms tightly together, clutching the information.

*Please don't die.*

Sven chased this away from his mind as quickly as it appeared, but he couldn't help but imagine his reserved spot next to Hannah at the cryonics facility. If anything were to happen, everything was in place.

And every time he closed his eyes, he thought of the jail cell, only slightly larger than a coffin.

The limo was half-way there. The tinted windows hid Sven from view and made the world a shade darker as he peered out. Traffic was light, and there was no one on the streets, like usual. Gray clouds rolled in threatening rain but had yet to deliver. Sven's nose crinkled at the smell of the big and sweaty guards. He wasn't about ready to ask to roll down a window. His legs fell asleep, but he stayed quiet.

Pulling into Charles' garage, the door shut, and everyone got out. The men stayed on either side of Sven as the driver pushed buttons to enter the fortress. Two left, and the other two escorted Sven to the office that Sven had been in before. Charles sat behind the desk, a scowl across his face.

He stood, waving to the men to leave. "Shut the door," he said, snappy, short, and stern. They did as instructed with a click of a lock behind them.

"Doctor Sven Olander, it is time for us to have a serious discussion about our arrangement, or lack thereof. What's in the briefcase?"

Sven cleared his throat, his heart pounding. "I was told to bring paperwork, and I did as you asked." Obviously, he knows. Charles pounded the top of his desk before Sven placed the briefcase there.

"You thought you could break into one of my facilities and get away with it?" Charles snapped open the briefcase, and seemingly happy with the contents, closed it, putting it next to him. "I know what you took." He rubbed his chin. "I can't say I blame you. With no proof, there isn't any reason for my motivation. I assume you had others to assist you in this 'heist', since you entered the jail with nothing but a transmitter. So, did you find anything in the paperwork that you were looking for?"

Sven paused, sweat gathering on his brow and in his armpits. Gripping the armrests of his chair, he said, "Well, I found out that you were doing research on what we talked about, but I haven't looked through everything yet."

"Of course not. You had just broken in yesterday." Charles narrowed his eyes. "I can't trust you, now more than ever, and I can't believe I am going to do this, but I must do away with your skepticism. I am going to show you my true motivation."

Sven's eyes darted in all directions. The click of the locked door flashed in his memory. *I shouldn't have broken in. Damn, that was dumb. There had to be another way. Is he going to feed me to a room full of mutants? Have those brawny men come back and take care of me in a slow, painful manner? Or is he serious?*

Charles stood. "Stay right next to me." The door clicked open after he hit a button on his desk, Charles taking the briefcase with him. Sven prayed he wasn't going to a torture chamber. Charles and Sven exited the room and started down the hall. They passed many doors, all of them closed, until they came to a set of stairs that cascaded down. Sven pictured falling down the stairs, either from Charles pushing him or his own nervousness. Clasping his hands in an effort to control his jitters, he used the railing on the way down, staying right next to Charles.

At the bottom of the stairs was one of the biggest libraries Sven had ever seen. While most of Charles' mansion was dark, his library had white shelves and bright-colored books filling them. Paintings of waterfalls and a clear ocean that Sven hadn't seen since he was a boy displayed on the walls. A plush oversized chair of a vibrant red sat in the corner, easily the oldest piece of furniture in the house.

Charles took a book off the shelf, *The DNA of our Ancestors*, followed by a pop like a latch being unhinged. Sven jumped at the sound.

The bookcase was masking a door, which Charles opened once he found the groove. Sven rubbed his arm to warm himself from the cool air that escaped. "Stay right beside me," Charles reminded him, entering the passageway and shutting the door behind him.

Swallowed in darkness until Charles hit a light switch, they found themselves in another hallway. The walls, floor, and ceiling were all black. Sven felt he was walking into nothingness. They walked in silence. Where were they going?

Entering another room, a low hum of ceiling fans cut through the air. The same size as the entryway of his house, it was mainly void except for an unmistakable chamber in the far corner.

Two cryogenic chambers.

Now he was holding Hannah for some kind of ransom? What was this? His jaw dropped in disbelief, moving closer to the chamber without saying a word until he realized the figures were much too small to be Hannah. Sven's eyes were steadfast at the child-size figures in the chambers, and imagined Lucas there instead of his present spot at the small land he purchased close to home. With a short intake of breath, his eyes tightly shut until he willed the thought away.

They reopened.

Charles' breathing grew shallow, his eyes downcast until they raised to the first chamber. Blinking a multitude of times, Sven wondered if he would even notice if he walked away. When Charles put his hand on the glass, he could only see an outline of the person in the murky solution.

"My daughter, Kimberly. Her life shouldn't end so early. She fell out of a tree that I created on a special playground for her to be safe. Landing on her head the way that she did, they could do nothing. But me, I can. I won't lose the most important person in the world to me."

Sven couldn't take his eyes off of Charles, and his words were so familiar. They were the same thoughts that had been running through his head since he had lost Hannah. *Maybe we aren't so different. Could his persona be all a front and he's not the greedy bastard I took him for?*

As if reading his thoughts, Charles said, "I'm not a monster. I just want my little girl back, and if my money can bring her back, it's the best thing I've ever done with it. To hell with the rest of the world."

He had Sven's attention until the very last statement. The rest of the world could go to hell, but wasn't Sven considering the same thing? What would he do in his situation? His head pounded in the right frontal lobe as he wondered how many mutants would spread at the price of this little girl living? At the price of Hannah living? Could he trust him?

At least now he had more understanding.

"What do you want from me? Not to say anything and let you take all the serum?" Sven paused, looking over at Kimberly again. "I'm sorry about your daughter."

"Don't be sorry. Help me save her."

For the first time, Sven didn't see a billionaire tycoon trying to rule the world, but a father trying to save his daughter.

"What exactly are you asking? To turn the other way when you take all the serum? For how long? Until you find a cure for dying?" Even as Sven said it, it sounded strange. He had never thought of it in those terms until now.

"Yes! To find a cure for dying. That is exactly what we're doing." Charles' down demeanor flipped to an excited child on Christmas. He stood straight up and smiled.

"Who's in this one?" Sven asked, pointing to the other chamber, a body about the same size as Kimberly.

"An orphan that died. We would want to test it on someone else before our loved ones, right? The boy is no worse off if it isn't successful."

*My heart is telling me, take the deal! He gets Kimberly back, I get Hannah back, and all is good. But what about the rest of the world? If resurrecting them will take all the serum, what will happen to the world that they are coming back to? We will find another way. Another cure. Can I trust that he would share his findings?*

Charles paced the floor, never letting his eyes wander off his daughter. "So, you have two options. You either take my side and quit meddling in my plan, letting me take all the serum I need from the tree frogs, or you interfere and I will handle it. You will no longer be a threat to me or anyone. Permanently. And you can forget about the chamber next to Hannah that you reserved. Both of the Olander chambers will stop working." He clicked his tongue on the roof of his mouth. "And that will be the end of both of you. Forever."

Sven swallowed the lump in his throat.

"You don't have to answer me now or ever. If I see you or know of you meddling in my plans, you won't ruin them." Charles smiled. "I will make it look like an accident. There are mutants everywhere and as you know, security is at an all-time low. That's just something to keep in mind."

Sven didn't say a word, just nodded, and wondered what else he had in his secret room. How many rooms were there? The property was massive.

"And I will see you out." Charles smiled and placed his hand on Kimberly's chamber once again, whispering something that Sven couldn't hear. They returned the exact way they came, and Charles said, "it's such a pity. If you would have trusted me a little more, you would know everything that's in here." He patted the side of the briefcase with force.

Sven wished he could see past the exterior of that briefcase and see what else was inside.

# CHAPTER TWENTY-ONE

"I wonder what this is going to be about?" asked Sven, catching up with Adam and Jesse in the hall. "Why would Josh want to meet with just us?" He jittered with nervousness. Like he wasn't stressed out enough from his visit with Charles.

"I guess we'll find out," said Jesse. "As long as he isn't reprimanding us. We're doing a great job around here lately, and you know how hard it is to keep treating the patients and the junkies. He is nothing like Daniel, and I mean AT ALL."

"Welcome back to work, Sven. Where were you yesterday?" asked Adam. He sounded like a parent of a teenager.

"Sick, but I feel much better now." Adam gave him a sideways look, but left it alone. Sven wondered how he was going to explain the missing paperwork.

"Good to hear." Changing gears he said, "As far as Josh reprimanding us, I try to be respectful, and treat all the patients the same, but it's hard to have the same respect for someone that has done this to themselves." Adam quickened his step. "If that's wrong, so be it." They all moved faster as it neared noon. Sven agreed Josh would be the type to value punctuality.

They made it to the conference room, one of the smallest in the building of four. Josh was already there, and he got up to greet them as they entered. "It's so nice that everyone could come at this short notice," said Josh. "I wanted to go over a few things today." He straightened the vest of his suit, and Sven remembered Josh wearing black the last time he met him. Did the man not have any other suits?

"First, I would like to clarify why I am here, in case any of you have been misinformed. The merge of the old Black Hills facility and the present one is a monumental task so I can take care of more of the details with this and the continuation of the patient care remains at its peak performance, if not better."

Notes of Julia's recent progression appeared on the wall. She had been doing better, but still had flashes of anxiety. "I think it's time that we removed her chip. It's the safest it's ever going to get, and the benefits will largely outweigh the risks."

"What risks are we talking about?" asked Adam.

"You should know the risks of any operation," said Josh briskly. "The highest risk of all, of course, is she could expire, but she could have other health conditions. If it is successful, with the right dosage of the serum, after a number of months I think she could be a normal member of society, after a full psychiatric evaluation."

"That would be amazing. No doubt with me here, she'll be back to normal in no time. I've got the skills," said Jesse, pushing back his shoulders as he puffed out his chest.

Sven pulled his head back and shook his head. There goes that new arrogance showing up again. "She's been here for so long. WE are ready to do whatever it takes to make her well."

Adam looked from one man to the other, darting a look at Jesse to warn him of the eye roll he started. Jesse turned serious, clearing his throat. Josh went through all the procedures they would need and the scheduling so they all could be there.

"One other thing, gentleman. When there are any changes in the patients, I want to be notified. I have included new special reports that are to be filled out when this occurs. If it is of a more dire nature, I am to be notified immediately." *Oh, great. More paperwork. Less time with the patients. Less time to take down Charles.* "Good luck to all of you. I will be there on Friday before Julia's procedure to make sure everything is prepared correctly. That's all for today. There are patients we need to take care of." As the three scientists were getting up to leave, Josh said, "and if there is a problem with any of the patients, they stay in this facility. I hope I have made myself clear."

"Loud and clear," said Sven.

"Good." The other men nodded, and if they could have gotten out there any faster, they would have.

"Well, that went well," said Jesse, as they were leaving and Josh was still in the conference room closing up his computer.

"He just wants everything to go well," said Sven. "Wait until we get to know him. He might not be so bad." He hoped.

"As long as we stay on our best behavior. I still find it strange he happened to show up all of a sudden after we took Jill down," said Jesse. "Whoever captured him just decided to let him go?"

None of them had answers.

— • —

# Chapter Twenty-Two

Sven entered Jill's room, where she was snoring softly. Glad, knowing that it would be easier to administer the serum, he crept inside and watched her. Jill's breathing was even and steady, her heart rate normal, and her blood pressure well within range. Tremors traveled her body. Must have been a nightmare, he reasoned, as he went to dose the spidomed. He wondered if she regretted experimenting on herself with such dire consequences. Had her mind wrapped around what she had done, or was her psyche too far gone to understand the serious repercussions?

Dosing the spidomed, he administered the serum, not taking his eyes off of her to make a mental note to record her reactions on the computer. Her tremors turned into convulsions in seconds.

"Code Red!" he called out after hitting the button next to the monitor, his voice echoing through the halls, the system automatically entering the room number 204. Being cuffed to the bed because of the charges brought against her helped her from injuring herself. Doctors poured into the room, surrounding Sven in a sea of white. Her heart rate and respirations sped up as her piercing scream filled the air. Everyone stepped aside while a doctor pushed in a machine that sandwiched her bed in the middle. It could breathe for her and shock her heart into a rhythm at the same time. A deafening beeping came from it, showing all the vitals that were off.

Josh entered, his face twisted with anger at seeing Sven with a spidomed in his hands. Slamming Sven against the wall knocked the wind out of him. The spidomed went flying. Josh gripped the lapel of Sven's lab coat in tight fists. "What did you do to her?"

"Nothing!" Sven lifted his hands in surrender. "I just got in here."

"Well, you must have done something." Two of the other doctors pulled Josh off of him.

"What do you think you're doing?" asked one.

"You're not helping," said the other. "You should be here for your niece instead of taking it out on Dr. Olander."

Jill's convulsing had stopped, her eyeball moving rapidly underneath the lid. Josh rushed over to her, unable to be too close to interfere with the machine. "Damn, damn, damn," Josh whispered. Sven caught his breath, straightening his coat. Fluorescent green numbers showing her vitals read on the side of the machine on a black screen, constantly changing with Jill's body.

Her heart rhythm returned to normal, along with everything else, in a matter of minutes.

"Oh, thank God," said Josh, moving closer to Jill after they pulled the machine out. Jill was back asleep, but this time, soundly. Many of the doctors filed out of the room with only a few remaining.

"Do you two need us?" one doctor asked.

"I think we have it," said Sven, giving a sideways glance at Josh and keeping his distance. "Thank you." The scientists left, taking the machine with them.

Josh stared down at Jill, holding her hand so gingerly as if it might break. "I can't believe you did this to yourself. I should have been here when you needed me. This is all my fault." He gripped the edge of the bedrail, leaning his head down with an exasperated sigh. "That was so close."

Sven crept closer to Josh, and Josh jumped as if he had forgotten that Sven was there. Footsteps echoed in the hallway right before Jesse and Adam entered the room.

"What happened here?" asked Adam, seeing Josh's panicked state and Sven's haggard appearance.

"I heard code red. She looks pale," said Jesse with an indifferent expression, like he was talking about the color of wallpaper.

"We obviously need to adjust the serum," said Adam. "If she's getting too much, her body might not handle it."

"If she gets too little, it won't do the job that it needs to do," said Sven. "I say cut it in half starting tomorrow and see what happens."

"Don't forget to document that. We don't want any mix-ups," replied Adam.

Josh flipped around, his eyes narrowed as he said, "There better not be any mix-ups."

"You know the serum is new, and it has different effects on everyone," said Jesse. "Why don't you just focus on yourself? You can't help her if you don't." He moved closer to Josh, and Sven shook his head. He stayed ready for a fight. "How much sleep have you gotten lately? No disrespect, but you look like hell."

Sven gave him a warning glance.

"What is that supposed to mean?" Josh seethed, tension in his stance, veins protruding from his neck, and his right eye twitched.

"Just that you have to take care of your health first," Jesse muttered.

"I take care of my family first."

Sven made a broad step in between them, placing his hands up on either side. "This is neither the time nor the place."

"Sven's right," said Adam. "We are all supposed to be on the same side."

"We can be on the same side and have a difference of opin-ion. Don't worry. I'm fine," Jesse snapped back. "I have other patients to see." In seconds, he was out the door.

"He just doesn't understand," said Josh, going back to Jill's bedside, where she continued to sleep. "The last time I saw Daniel, we had this big argument about Jill. There was some-thing about her that just wasn't right. I thought she should talk to someone, but Daniel firmly believed that there would be nothing wrong with anyone in our family." He hung his head. "I loved my brother. I hate to think that is my last memory of him."

Sven thought of his argument with Nathan, glad that they had come to an understanding and made up.

"I wonder what would have happened if I would have been here after Daniel died. I could have gotten her help." Sven and Adam listened, and with how he was talking, Sven wondered if he was thinking out loud or if he remembered they were in the room.

"And maybe it wouldn't have made a difference at all," said Adam.

"Maybe." There was a faraway look in his eyes.

"We'll never know. It's time to move forward," said Adam.

Josh glared at him before his eyes softened. "Maybe it wouldn't have made a difference. Now I have to live with never knowing. Just like when I lost Daniel, it's time to move on. That's what my big brother would have wanted. I am finishing what he started by making sure there is some end to this nightmare."

Sven picked up the spidomed off the floor, moving to the nearby sink to clean it, feeling like he had some understanding now where Josh was coming from and why he was so abrasive. Josh was making amends with a ghost. As for the moving on, he was unable to meet Josh's eyes. He wasn't about ready to give up on Hannah and was in no mood to get a lecture from Adam about it. It was different with Hannah and Daniel. Daniel was now with his wife in the next life, while he was stuck here with no one. Lost in thoughts, he continued to scrub the spidomed far beyond clean.

"We'll go," said Adam, "and give you some time with her." He cleared his throat, and Sven put the spidomed back in the drawer.

"She should be better tomorrow," said Sven to Adam as they continued to walk down the hall.

— • —

# CHAPTER TWENTY-THREE

J ulia's room was spotless. She clasped her hands tightly in her lap, biting her bottom lip. They had machinery on either side of her to update her, nothing having to touch her skin. Adam stood by the head of the bed before Julia opened her eyes. "Are you ready for this?" he asked her.

"I think so. You mean, after this I might be able to be...like you?" Tears welled up in her eyes, as did the other scientists in the room. Jesse and Adam surrounded her bed, wishing her all the best.

"That's the plan," said Adam, reaching out to touch her hand. "It might take some time afterwards, but you could leave this place and live a normal life."

"Wow." Julia laid back underneath the covers, her body more relaxed than before. Shoulders dropped and fingers unclenched, closed her eyes.

Josh peeked his head into the room. "Is she sedated yet?"

"Not yet," said Adam. "Give us five minutes."

Josh walked over to the near-sleeping mutant young lady that had gone through so much. "Julia..." She opened her eyes, the fierce green fading in the dimly lit room. "You don't worry, we are going to take good care of you. Do you understand me?" Her head bobbed up and down without saying a word, closing her eyes once more.

"And maybe..." she said faintly, "someday I will be able to go outside again."

Josh didn't say a word, but there was something sad in his face just then. Pity or skepticism, Sven couldn't tell. Perhaps both. But it was nice Josh was showing some kind of feeling. Josh patted her on the arm and instructed the men to be down in the operating room within the next fifteen minutes.

Adam placed the sedation patch on her arm with adhesive, and in less than a minute, she was out. Sven remembered the time when they had to use IVs and needles to sedate someone for surgery, glad those days were gone. The patch worked so much faster, too, and with less chance of infection or allergy. She looked so peaceful, and he remembered the last time she had an outburst. Waking from a nightmare she thought was real, Julia thought that the whole building was under attack. Strangely enough, someone was breaking into the facility, so she was close. The serum was under attack, and it was time for him to protect it.

"I think she's out," said Jesse. "I'd give her five minutes, and we could take her downstairs."

"It's so nice having all this extra space after getting Black Hills," said Adam, referring to the wing of Juniper Ridge that was once controlled by Jill. "And we have more operating rooms as well. Four is far better than two." He looked down at his patient. "She has been waiting such a long time."

"Isn't she the longest human patient we have?" asked Jesse.

"Yes, still living," said Sven, taking her vitals before heading down to surgery and connecting all the medical devices to her via patch number two. As long as she stayed within ten feet of the devices, they would all register correctly. He thought of the tubes and lines that had to be connected to the patient, and was glad the cumbersome things were gone, especially during transport. Getting her down to the room would be so much easier. "Everything looks great. Her blood pressure couldn't be more in range, temperature fine. She's ready."

Sven opened the door wide as Adam pushed her through, Jesse staying close behind with the cordless monitors in constant watch to her well-being.

The men traveled in silence down the hall and to the elevators, traveling down to the main floor in the back of the building where the operating rooms were. The mutants were their noisy selves: a bird cawed, an ape grunted, and Sven could swear he heard a girl weeping. It was possible, but he was hearing from far away because the animals were only on the first floor. Impressed with his hearing at such an advanced age, he knew being a doctor it was a necessity to be sharp with his hearing, sight, hands, and mind. They had no time to think slowly, because anything could happen at any moment.

Before entering the operating room, all scientists removed their gloves and rewashed their hands, putting on masks to cover their nose and mouth. Before they entered the room, they put on surgical caps for their hair and washed their hands again along with the assistant, Kate. Everyone wore gloves.

"Two hours?" confirmed Sven to Adam.

"That's how long she will be out. We have to be fast, efficient, and careful. Let me see your hands." Sven and Jesse put out their hands. No one trembled. "Okay, I think we can proceed."

Sven watched the monitors as Adam sterilized Julia's head, going in on the right side where there was no hair. They removed it when they inserted the chip, and it never grew back. Sven couldn't believe that they didn't remove the chip when the problems began, but it was too dangerous. Inserted to watch her brain activity and thought process, it was not a success, but just caused more harm than good.

Kate handed Adam a tri-saw. The tri-saw was a tool that they used in surgeries that only went as deep as necessary to go through the skull. The microscopic cutting caused healing in a fraction of the time and less pain when the person awoke. All sterilized instruments were in pristine condition.

Adam took a deep breath, and Sven nodded to him to proceed. Glancing at the monitors, Jesse promised he was keeping an eye on everything. Adam cut into the skull with ease and precision. Everything stabilized, he split open the skull as it made a cracking sound. Sven helped him keep it open until they could attach a splitter to keep it agape, covering the rest of her head as they turned her head to find the chip.

Sven asked Kate for the tweezers, wide at the top that narrowed down to a pinpoint. He got the microchip, so tiny and sandwiched well within the brain, and dropped it in a petri-dish on an adjoining table. They really got it out. It was there so long, and now her life was going to be changed forever, hopefully for the better.

"Well done, doctor," said Sven.

"We are doing great." Jesse stared up at the monitors again, but his jaw went slack. "Um...we may have a problem." The monitor beeping amplified. Sven and Adam's attention traveled to the monitors. "Her heart rate, it's dropping."

Adam rushed to the adjoining cart, the spidomeds spread across the top and ready for anything. He handed Sven the purple one filled with Notifou that speeds up the heart rhythm, but after administering it, her heart rate slowed more.

"Paddles!" Adam yelled, and Sven grabbed the defibrillator from his side, charging it up to the proper joules before attaching them to her chest and pulling the trigger. Her chest jumped, but her heart rate did not.

"Shit! Shit!" said Jesse. "More Notifou." He grabbed another spidomed before Sven jumped in.

"Stop! One more will kill her." Sven reached down to give CPR, breathing for her as Adam continued with the paddles. They looked up.

The heartbeat was slowing even more. She was almost legally dead.

"We're losing her," said Adam.

"I am NOT losing anyone today." Sven continued to breathe into her lungs as they counted, Adam shocking her.

Jesse gripped the spidomed. "Don't you think…"

"No, Jesse!" Just as he was about ready to attach it to her arm to administer the drugs, the monitor's beep grew quiet. Her heartbeat was rising, and her breathing was coming back to normal. Sven hooked her up to oxygen and fought the spinning of his head. She was okay.

"Let's sew her back up as quick as we can. We need to mitigate the risk of infection," said Adam. Sven lasered her incision. It would heal quickly; it had to. Exhausted, he shook with fury. This was supposed to go smoothly.

The doctors returned her to her room to recover, watching her closely on the monitors. Someone came in every few minutes to see her.

"Jesse, I need to talk to you." Sven's voice was deep and deliberate. "Now."

"What?" They leaned in the hallway outside Julia's room, Jesse's arms crossed in front of him. "What did I do?"

"What did you do? You almost killed her. When I tell you to do something, or to not do something, you listen to me. Do you understand me?" Sven's temple pulsed.

Jesse put his hands on his hips before flying them into the air. "I was just trying to save her life."

"That would have killed her, and you know it. Don't you ever defy me like that again, especially in the operating room. I have been doing this a little longer than you have." Sven's face was red, his fists tight against his side. "I have a hell of a lot more experience. People's lives are at stake."

"I'm not a loser and you know it would have worked just as well. You know I'm right."

"I never said you were a loser, and WE stopped Jill. You just happened to be the one that stabbed her in the back. Get off your high horse and go do Julia's vitals, and just her vitals."

"Got it." Jesse turned on his heel with a sigh and an eye roll, going back to Julia's room.

Adam came down the hall with the magic serum in hand. "Ready for her first dose. Think you were a little hard on him?"

"You heard that?"

"I'm sure the entire building heard that, but I have noticed he's getting full of himself. I better get Julia her serum so she can start healing," Adam said before he turned back to Sven.

"He probably needed to hear that. Maybe it'll make him think." Sven wished.

"I hope so. If you can handle this, I'll talk to you later. I'll be in my office, okay?"

"I'm good," said Adam.

Sven passed by Jill's room on his way to his office and heard Josh's voice. Leaning into the door, but trying not to be too obvious, he heard Josh say, "Jill, I'm here now. I'm sorry for not being here, but I told you why I wasn't."

"Maybe you didn't try enough." Her voice sounded different to Sven. Less brash, more to understand.

"I told you about my capture. Why did you do what you did? That is the more important question." *He should have loved her enough to not leave in the first place, thought Sven. Love can do anything, and there's no making up for that now.*

Sven lost his footing, and his shoulder slipped into the wall. Straightening himself up, Josh became quiet. *Damn it, I blew it.* Sven pulled away from the door and was about ready to head back down the hall right before Josh poked his head out.

Damn, it would have been nice to know what she said. Why did she do it? Maybe another day.

Sven closed the door to his office and locked it. Picking up his pictures on his desk one by one, his wife, his friends, he put his head between his knees and took a few deep breaths. God, that was close. It could have gone so differently. Now Julia can heal.

*I can't lose anyone else. I don't think I could take it.* Flashes of Julia close to death filled his mind. He had to remind himself that he didn't really lose Hannah, not for forever. He will come back to her somehow.

# CHAPTER TWENTY-FOUR

S ven watched Julia sleep, still groggy from her surgery and the sedation. He checked her chart, perusing through the notes to look over past vitals and how she was healing. Julia had already received multiple doses of the serum, and although she was healing up okay, she would need more.

A lot more.

Sven went down to the lab with the medicines, remembering when someone had broken in. He pictured the broken beakers all over the floor, the serum that was spilt and wasted. This burglar could have risked Julia's life. If she doesn't get enough, he knows she will never recover. That's just not a possibility. Not after everything that she had been through.

He pulled up a chair, relaxing and put Julia's hand in his. Not usually this close to his patients, Julia was an exception. A long-time resident, she was one of the first human mutants that entered the facility. When she went to the cabin in the woods, hiding so they could try to find a cure until Jill could get to them, Adam had told Sven about when she had looked out the window, never seeing outside since she had spent most of her life in windowless Juniper Ridge. Her wonderment was magical, and he wanted to give that to her.

*So much we take for granted.*

Sven physically examined Julia and checked all her latest vitals, recording them before heading downstairs to the new storage room with the serum. He removed two of the vials, filling the spidomed with them. She would need a double dose, considering the single one has been so much help to her thus far and she would have excess healing to go through. "Please, I hope this is a good idea," he said to himself. Recording them in the log, he stepped aside when another doctor came in to take some medications. Sven watched him over his shoulder, trying to not be too obvious. The shortage of the serum had always made him watchful. The woman grabbed some antibiotics and smiled at Sven.

"Joselyn." She extended her hand. "I don't think we've formally met, but you are kind of a legend."

"I am?" Sven waved his hand in the air. "I don't do anything here that other doctors don't do."

"Don't be so modest. You've worked here a long time, Dr. Olander, and you've made a lot of progress. You and your team are amazing." Her brown eyes widened. "It gives all of us new doctors something to aspire to."

"Thank you."

"It was nice meeting you, but I should go. I have a patient that is waiting for this," she said, waving the antibiotics in the air.

"If you need anything, don't hesitate to ask," said Sven.

She smiled at him as she left.

On his way to Julia's room, he wanted to stop by and talk to Josh about her surgery and the amount of serum that she was going to need for recovery. Surprised to see his door was ajar, he was about ready to enter when he peeked in and noticed Josh hunched over his desk. His face was pale and ashen, his expression somber. Staring off into space, Sven spoke and broke his trance.

"Josh, can I talk to you?"

Josh jumped, standing up swiftly and running his foot into the wall.

"Of course."

"I didn't mean to startle you. I wanted to talk to you about Julia." Josh motioned for Sven to sit across from him.

Josh's office was still as simple as before, without one picture of family or any personal effects. Today it was frigid, and Sven wrapped his lab coat tighter around himself.

"Sorry," Josh said. "I run a little warm."

"No matter. It's better for the germs, right? Well, I wanted to talk to you about Julia's recovery. She's going to need more serum that we can give her. Is there any way that we can outsource and get it from somewhere else?"

"I'm looking into that. Since Julia just got out of surgery, I haven't seen her. I heard what happened and read it in her chart. How is she recovering from such trauma?"

"She's healing fine, for now. With light sedation, she doesn't seemed to be in any pain." Sven played back her heart rate slowing in his head and winced at the thought. "We are keeping a close eye on her heart rate and breathing. All have been in normal ranges since the surgery."

"Well, that's good news. When I see how close you are to Julia, I understand. It's about fixing what you broke."

Sven's face tilted in confusion. What on earth was he talking about?

"I know she was one mutant you snuck out of here, and I am sure that didn't help matters any."

Sven's face grew taunt, and he jetted out his chin. "That wasn't my fault. Taking her out there didn't make her any worse off than she was before. You don't understand. You weren't there. When I saw her out in the world, she saw the world with the wonderment of a child. I want her to be able to go out and live like the rest of us. Julia isn't like other mutants. People react to viruses in different ways, and she reacted so differently. Not violent like the other patients, she has special gifts. That's why they put the chip in her head. I was all for it at first, because I thought they were going to make her better because of it, but I was wrong."

"I've seen her violent." Josh shook his head. "I'm going to have to disagree with you on that one. I haven't even been here that long."

"Yeah, she's violent when she's scared or confused, and a part of that is because she doesn't know how to handle the 'gifts' she's been given as a mutant. I think if you were trapped and shackled down, operated on where someone put a chip in your brain to know every brainwave, you would all be a little crazy, too." Sven stood, wanting to kick Josh's desk. Josh was a superior, and even though he hadn't been there nearly as long as Sven, was a higher rank. "I shouldn't have to justify her actions to you. I think I should go." Just when he almost seemed like he was one of us. What a disappointment.

"I was just speaking my mind." Josh rose and opened up the office door. "It's been a long day. Maybe you should head home."

Sven exited, but had no intention of going home. What would be the point? There was no one there.

Returning to Julia's room, he sat next to her bedside. Sleeping soundly, he checked all her vitals. She must have been exhausted, sleeping through all the tests. Sven checked all the monitors, looked at all the histories, and she was improving. It was almost time for another dose of the serum.

Adam entered the dimly lit room and jumped when he noticed Sven was there. "What are you still doing here?" he asked.

"I thought you would have headed home by now. I just came in to give her the normal dose.

"I've got it," said Sven, snatching the precious cure from Adam, waving it in front of him. "You put this back downstairs." Adam took it and stepped back with a questioning look.

"Okay…You should have told me. I'm the one scheduled for administering it."

"Don't worry. I always record it. Besides, I'm staying here for the night. Someone should be watching her for at least twenty-four hours, more like a few days."

"But Sven, we have plenty of people here. That's why we have shifts. You should get your rest."

"I will once she gets better. Don't you worry. I will see you in the morning." Sven turned away from him, leaning over Julia. He placed the spidomed on her arm, both doses of the serum smoothly seeping into her body.

Looking defeated, Adam turned to leave. "Don't stay too long, my friend. If you get tired, go home. They have it handled."

"I got it," he said, tossing the spidomed into the cleaning basket.

He could hear Adam's footsteps down the hall, and after watching Julia, he pulled out a book from the corner shelf that he had left there for another long night at the hospital, watching patients having a rough time while they slept.

The book was just getting good. It was an Alexa Bordeaux novel, one of his all-time favorites. Ironically enough, in real life, Bordeaux ended up turning mutant and killed the founder of Juniper Ridge many years ago, a decade after her first bestseller.

But she didn't mean it, and she was still a great novelist, back in the day. In her novel, who killed the young girl that was snatched from her bed in the middle of the night? It had to be the older brother with all kinds of mental problems. Or it could be the creepy neighbor that takes walks in the middle of the night, alone. With the mutants around in the world, only a crazy person would do that.

He glanced around, shaking his head at himself. No one was here, and they weren't going to care if he looked. Flipping through over 200 pages, he reached almost the end and skimmed.

The other brother. He knew it! When he had more time to read, at least he had the satisfaction that he was right, and he placed it back on the shelf. At least Bordeaux didn't make it too obvious.

"Well, Julia, I'm going to stretch my legs a bit. You seem to be doing fine. Don't worry, dear. I won't be gone long." He squeezed her hand as he stood, taking a quick breath in the realization that he did the same thing with Hannah after visiting her in the morning during her illness before he went to work. Looking down, he saw Hannah, pale and thin, a slight smile as Hannah squeezed his hand back.

With one more look at her monitors, he sat back down until his eyes drooped. His head hanging forward, he fell asleep.

— • —

# CHAPTER TWENTY-FIVE

"Hey, Tom." Sven said to the security guard, handing him a steaming cup of coffee from the break room while sipping on one himself. "How are things going in here?"

Tom was sitting at the main desk, but his eyes weren't on the monitors. His chin was in his hand, elbow on the desk, eyes drooping...

"Fine." He snapped up, wiping the saliva from his chin. He reached out for the coffee like a gift from the gods. Taking a long, savory sip, he said, "sweet, just the way I like it."

"Four sugar cubes and a splash of milk. I remember. Do you mind?" Sven pointed to the open chair. After Sven had been working there for years, he was more than allowed in the security room. "Anything interesting on the monitors? Let's take a look." At least if he was in there, he could watch Julia and the rest of the facility.

Josh was gone, or at least he wasn't in his office. He wondered if Josh knew anything about Charles, but being new in the area, he doubted it. Adam was still checking on patients, the closest one to the front door. *Good. Be with your family. Go home.*

"It's pretty quiet," Tom said. "But that's a good thing. I'm tired of all the break-ins."

"Do you think it's an inside job?" asked Sven. *I wonder what would happen if Alexa wrote the story?*

"I don't think so. Just desperate people. I don't understand how they get in, though." Sven thought of the almost-sleeping Tom.

"No idea." He had to fight to not say anything about the drowsy Tom. Julia was sleeping, Adam was seeing the latest mutant bobcat/many other things, and then there was Jill.

What was Josh saying to her?

"Could you turn up the volume in this room?" asked Sven. Tom shrugged, then pushed a few buttons on the board, and Sven could hear the conversation.

"Jill, your Uncle Josh is going to make sure there are changes. Everything is going to be all right." Jill looked different from the last time he saw her. Hands that were once pointed daggers were human, and fingernails were growing. Once a hollowed face was full, and her skin was smooth instead of the scaly surface it once was. Looking more like the Jill he remembered when he worked with her father, Daniel, he smiled. And listened intently.

What changes was Josh talking about?

"I'll make sure you get everything you need. I know you don't believe me, but I have an insider source."

Her eyelids were drooping.

"Look, I have got to go. I should let you rest. I'll see you tomorrow, okay?"

By the time he was done with that sentence, she had already fallen asleep. Make sure she gets everything she needs? Does he have an insider source or was he just trying to make her feel better? Does he know Charles?

"Is everything all right?" Tom asked, sensing the tension.

"Yes, it's fine. You can turn the volume off now." Sven got up to leave. "Can we keep this between us? About what was going on in that room?"

"Sure," said Tom, oblivious of the significance, "as long as you don't tell them about me needing this." He held up his coffee cup.

"Your secret is safe with me."

Sven returned to Julia's room, where she slept. He thumbed through his book, looking for interesting scenes he missed, and fell asleep right next to her, the slow beeping of the machines lulling them both to sleep.

—·—

# Chapter Twenty-Six

Sven smiled at the sunlight streaming through his car window, putting on sunglasses. The weather was unusually sunny in November. Sven was feeling revitalized from going home after nodding off next to Julia's bed. With some sleep aids and a warm glass of milk, he was sleeping soundly in his own bed. "Wonder what's going on this morning?" he asked, turning on his MCS scanner to find out if there was any mutant activity. The members of the MCS also could handle other emergency calls when the mutants were at a lull. The red light glowed, the reception perfect as an urgent message sounded over the broadcast.

"All people around the block of 17th and Sycamore use extreme caution. Stay in your homes and have all security precautions in place. A mutant attack is at 1725 Sycamore..."

Sven's heart stopped, and his ears rang. Stepping on the gas, the sunlight was an unwanted distraction. He turned up the scanner.

"We have MCS in place and there are residents needing medical attention."

"Oh, God." Sven tried to stay calm. *The MCS were there to help, but did they get there fast enough? What kind of mutant was it?* The scanner wasn't giving him enough information. *What kinds of weapons do I have on me? Tranquilizer gun? Spidomed?* He took a deep breath to focus. He hoped they said the address wrong or he just didn't hear them correctly, hoping they would announce it again.

"Again, all MCS in the vicinity of 1725 Sycamore please respond," and they went off the air. The static was deafening.

1725 Sycamore. Jesse's address.

Maybe he had already left for work, or running late and is still in the house. Flashes of Jesse kicking some overgrown mutant away while he reached for his weapon sprung into his mind. He's a good fighter, he's strong, he kept telling himself. He always has a weapon with him. But some of those mutants are so strong. A primal snarling and growling snapped him from his thoughts. In the distance, he could see the flashing lights of the emergency personnel, the coned-off road and people yelling.

Sven pulled over, opening his glove box and grabbing his gun for such emergencies. He wasn't planning on tranquilizing anything that was so close to Jesse's house. Something more permanent came to mind.

"Jesse!" he yelled, stumbling to the scene, aware of his surroundings. "Jesse!"

"Excuse me, sir," said an officer near the cone entrance. "This is not a safe area. Stay outside of the perimeter."

Sven flashed his badge. "I'm looking for Jesse Stein. Is he all right?"

"Doctor," the officer said, "give me one minute. Of course, your medical assistance might be of great use here."

The officer went to hit a button on his watch when Sven sneaked past him. Another officer went to grab him, but let go when they both noticed the mutant subdued and being prepped for transport.

The creature towered over everyone at a good twenty feet, casting a shadow of epic proportions. It stood on two feet like a human, a mouthful of spiked teeth over three inches long, with saliva dripping onto the pavement. It stumbled in a daze as they used their paralyzer gun, giving them five minutes to secure it and take it away. The slanted eyes reflected off the light, giving it a cat's eye-sheen. Black skin like a hairless dog covered its body, and a tail forked at the end whipped in all directions.

It fell.

Convinced the mutant wasn't a harm, Sven frantically searched the area for Jesse, running to the professionals on the scene to find information. Paramedics gathered in front of Jesse's house in a circle. Three crouched down, trying to help someone. Blood soaked the ground.

"Sven..." he heard a whimper, and his heart sank. He knew it.

"I'm right here." Sven knelt down to Jesse. Claw marks embedded across his right cheek from eye to ear, blood dripping on the ground. His right foot twisted at an awkward angle, resting on the pavement. But the paramedics were putting pressure on a wound on his right side, where it looked like the creature took a bite.

Sven instantly pressed against his side.

"Sir, we have it handled. Besides, you shouldn't be doing this without gloves."

"I don't care," said Sven. "I'm here."

Jesse smiled, then winced at the wound on his cheek. "It's all my fault. I should have been more careful."

"Nonsense. You just hang in there."

"Don't tell Lily," Jesse said. "She'll just worry." Lily was Jesse's older sister that was attending college at Duke University.

Jesse's face paled. The bleeding on his side slowed to a stop.

"I'm a doctor," explained Sven. "I can help." They wrapped a dressing around the wound and prepared the ambulance, making sure all of his vitals were good.

Screams filled the air. Sven stood to see the creature had woken up, breaking all of his restraints.

"Persistent, aren't you?" said Sven, standing up, but staying still right near Jesse. The creature grew closer, and Sven pulled his gun, shooting him in the gut. He growled and charged at them and Sven just kept shooting, one landing in his arm, one in his eye. The officers and MCS were throwing spidomeds and fires were being shot from tranquilizer guns and firearms. The creature collapsed right next to the group that was helping Jesse.

"I think that's the end of him," said Sven, still wanting them to take care of him as soon as possible.

Sven climbed into the ambulance after confirming, yes, he was a family member. At the back window of the ambulance, he watched them put the body of the mutant in the MCS rig, not letting go of Jesse's hand for a second. If there isn't enough serum to go around, could this happen again with someone else I love? The thought of this happening again made him shiver. He looked down at Jesse's eyes fluttering to stay awake, and he said, "I'm here. Everything is going to be okay." Jesse squeezed his hand.

## CHAPTER TWENTY-SEVEN

Sven pushed his chair closer to the hospital bed, grabbing onto the arms and leaning forward. He thought of Julia's surgery and how harshly he had reprimanded Jesse. If that had been the last time he had seen him…his thoughts interrupted when Jesse's eye fluttered open, the other hidden beneath a sterile gauze.

Sven's fingers laced together, joining his hands as if in prayer.

"Where am I?" Jesse asked. "What happened?"

"You're in the hospital," said Sven with a sigh of relief. "You're going to be just fine. How do you feel?"

"Stiff." Jesse twisted his body to stretch and let out a yelp. "What the hell? My side is killing me."

"You don't remember?" Sven hoped he wouldn't remember everything, because after seeing the shape that Jesse was in when he showed up, he imagined how it must have been to be attacked like that. The mutant was one of the worst that he had ever seen. He turned his attention back to Jesse. "Do you need some more pain medication?"

"No, I just won't move that way." He groaned. "Ever." Jesse reached up to touch his face where the bandage was and held it there. Narrowing his eye, he looked into the distance, then titled his head. "Oh, yeah, I remember, all right. My damn motion activator outside the garage must have been down when I went out to the car. When I opened that garage door…" He let out a shutter, moving up in bed, and winced.

"We don't have to rehash that now. You just rest," said Sven, putting his hand on Jesse's shoulder to get him to relax and lie back down.

"It dragged me out of the car, Sven," urged Jesse. "It's like the thing had human hands." Sven remembered the long, bony fingers of the creature, set up similar to human hands except for the extended claws. He could see how this could happen. But to have that ability in an animal mutant was unheard of.

"They are getting uncontrollable." Jesse's blood pressure rose, and the monitor blinked red, starting a constant ding.

"Jesse, we will take care of all of this," said Sven, one eye wandering to the monitor. "You focus on healing."

A nurse walked in, tall and thin, with red glasses and black hair tied up in a ponytail. Checking the monitors and turning it to reset, she asked Jesse, "How are you feeling? Do you need anything for the pain?"

"No."

She leaned back, surveying him and giving him a minute. "Are you sure? What's your pain level? Give me a number."

Jesse shifted again and winced. "Well, maybe it wouldn't hurt."

"I'm Jennifer, your nurse, and if you need anything, you just push this button," she explained, pointing to the button on the side of the bed. "I'll be right back. Give you some time to visit with your dad."

Jennifer left as quickly as she arrived, which gave Jesse a chance to ask. "My dad?"

"Well, they wouldn't let me ride with you unless I was family, and they didn't really have time to look into it."

"No, that's cool." Jesse smiled, then winced at the movement in his face. "Dad." Jesse stared off into space, then said, "And about Julia's surgery..."

"Lesson learned," said Sven. "You're both okay, and that's what matters."

There was a knock on the open door where Adam was standing. "I just heard what happened. How are you feeling?" Adam stood on the other side of Jesse, giving him a once over before checking all the monitors.

"I've been better." He pointed to his face. "This is going to leave a scar."

"At least you're alive. It could have been a lot worse. I heard about your side. Did they wrap it correctly?" Adam moved the covers aside on Jesse's right side, and Jesse pushed his hands away.

"Stop that! I'm just fine." Jesse winced at the movement.

"Sorry." He stepped away, but still stared at his blanket as if being able to see through it.

"You're not Doctor Davidson here. You're Adam, my friend, and a *visitor*."

"Got it." Adam pulled up a chair next to Sven. "How the heck could this happen?"

"I've already told it once," snipped Jesse, rolling his eyes at the tame language. "And Sven caught the aftermath. Why don't you ask him?"

"It was lucky I was nearby," explained Sven, telling Adam what happened when he heard the scanners and everything that Jesse had told him.

"The mutant opened his door? I've never heard of a mutant that could do something like that, especially a non-human one." Adam rolled his shoulders and popped his knuckles, all joints cracking with each movement. "They're getting worse, even with the serum out there. Could the virus be getting stronger instead of weaker? Could it fight against the serum and the serum stop working?"

"I think it's just the fact that we need all the serum that we can get," explained Sven. "The lax security around this town doesn't help the situation." He worried about Charles' work with the serum, how much it would take to bring their departed back.

"I know what it's like, and it won't happen to me again." Adam eyed the glass of water that Sven had been sipping on with revulsion. "I will work night and day, so I won't return to that monster."

"We need to work together and get this under control, making sure the tree of life is attainable. Charles Williams can't have control over it," said Sven.

"That's right. That son of a bitch is just trouble. We need to figure out an attack plan." Jesse fidgeted in his bed. Without saying a word, Sven could see the pain on his scrunched face.

"And we will," agreed Sven. "But first, where is that nurse?" Sven went to the door to peer down the hall when he spotted another nurse leading Lily and Jesse's neighbor, Mr. Sandalson, into Jesse's room.

"Not too much longer," she warned the visitors. "The patient needs to get some rest and it's getting full in here."

"Where are his pain medications?" demanded Sven.

"She should be back any moment," said the nurse. "And I can trust you will all be just a few more minutes?" They all nodded like they were being scolded. Adam had calmed down for the time being.

"Lily, how did you get here so fast?" Jesse straightened in his bed and smiled.

She rushed over to him, about ready to hug him, but stopped when she saw the bandages. With tears in her eyes, she asked, "what happened to you?" Before giving him a chance to answer, she said, "I was going to surprise you for your birthday, but when I showed up I saw all the..." Pausing, she said, "I'm just glad you're okay. I love you."

"I love you, too, Lily. I'm fine, really." Sven stood so she could sit next to her brother. Jesse relaxed and Sven knew Lily was the pain medicine that Jesse needed all along. "My birthday isn't until next month, and what about school?"

"Ah, I'm on break, and next month is next week."

Jesse paused, looking up at the air. "Oh, I guess it is. You're doing so well in your classes, I wouldn't want to screw that up just for having a birthday," he teased. His face turned somber. "Mom and Dad would be really proud of you, like I am."

"They would be proud of you, too, Doctor," she boasted. "We'll always have each other."

"Thank God for that." He leaned his head back against the pillows. Sven thought he was going to fall asleep, but he lifted his head again. "Sometimes I forget, I guess. I couldn't save Mom and Dad, but I have you. I think I have to go through all of this stuff on my own, but I never have to. I'm one of the lucky ones." He let out a yawn. "Thanks for bringing her, Mr. Sandalson. I appreciate it. Did any of you ever meet my neighbor?"

"I'm just glad you're okay." He spoke quietly and stayed by the door of the crowded room.

"Don't be shy. He was the one that told me I should be a doctor."

"Didn't take an Einstein to know that," said the man. "I remember when you were in high school and volunteered at the animal shelter. That's when we didn't understand the mutant situation and thought they were just sick. You always wanted to fix everything and make everything better."

"Your encouragement meant a lot to me," said Jesse.

"Animals and music," agreed the neighbor. "You were always playing that guitar. I remember one night Millie was complaining it was too loud." He laughed. "I sat in the living room and listened. You were really good."

Jennifer interrupted by peeking her head in the door. "My, we have a roomful. Sorry it took so long. We had an emergency and I was pulled away." Lily gave her a sour look while Jesse nudged her in the arm.

"Excuse me," she said, gingerly moving Jesse's arm from the covers and placing the spidomed on his arm. "This should work in seconds."

"When is the doctor coming in?" asked Sven. "I have a few questions."

She glanced at the clock. "He finished his rounds and is about ready to go home, but I can let him know you would like to speak with him."

"I would appreciate that," he said, noticing Jesse looked more relaxed already. His eyes would be wide open, then shut.

"No need to fight it," said Sven. "Rest promotes healing. I will come back and check on you," he promised.

"Yeah, I need to get going, too," said Adam. "You just take care of yourself."

"I'm just running to the cafeteria to grab a coffee. I will be back," said Lily, putting her hand on his arm. "Get some sleep."

Jesse nodded in agreement.

Jennifer documented his pain med into the computer and made sure Jesse had his call light available before dimming the lights and leaving. Even in the downcast lights, Sven noticed Jesse's lingering gaze on Jennifer.

"Remember," Sven said, patting Jesse on the shoulder, "girls dig scars. Good night."

"Good night," Jesse mumbled, asleep before the two men left the room.

Out in the hall, Sven spotted Lily, back against the wall, face bent down as she gripped the bridge of her nose, sniffling. "I got this one," he told Adam, patting him on the back.

"I'll go find the doctor," said Adam, "and get us an update." Lily didn't even notice when Adam walked by.

"Hey," said Sven, easing up to her. He put his hand on her shoulder. "He's going to be all right. Your brother is a tough one."

Without saying a word, she reached out to him and held on, crying in his chest. Sven leaned over to a nearby ledge and handed her a tissue. "I know," she said, taking a deep breath. "Thank you. You're a good friend. I'm glad Jesse has you when I'm not here."

"The feeling is mutual. Would you like some company?"

"I think I just want some time to myself to take it all in, ya know?" she said, dabbing her eyes with the tissue before blowing her nose.

"I understand." Sven watched her until she took the elevator to the cafeteria, and on his way out he wondered what would happen if Charles goes through with his plan. With less serum for the mutants, will all the hospitals be filled with their victims?

— · —

# CHAPTER TWENTY-EIGHT

Sven took the long trek to the bottom floor in search of Adam, refusing to use the elevators the entire way. It was imperative that he stayed in the best shape that he could. After two floors down and walking down the long hallways to the other part of the building, he took the elevator to the floor underneath the first floor, panting and trying to regain his breath. "I'm just jumping from one hospital to the other," he said, thinking of the ten-minute visit he had with Jesse that morning before he promptly fell asleep.

Surprised not to see Adam, but Josh, his steps slowed. *I shouldn't be surprised to find him down here. He's a supervisor here.* Josh wasn't taking any of the serum. Sven stayed quiet, watching him through the doorway as Josh yanked on the doors of the serum without putting in his fingerprint. Josh pulled on the sides with substantial force, but nothing moved. He began going through the supplies next to the refrigerators.

"What are you doing?" asked Sven, walking into the room.

Josh jumped, clutching his chest. "You scared me. I was just gathering some supplies."

"Well, if you have patients today, don't forget the serum." He gave Josh a questioning look. Did he even know what he was doing?

"About the serum. Have we got it right with Jill? I don't want her to get too much and have something happen like the other day. I don't want her to get too much and become an addict, either. Then we have a whole new battle."

"She's doing better, yes. Read her notes."

"Since you're here, I figured I would just ask you."

"Yes, she's doing fine. Improving a little at a time. Go up and see her yourself."

Josh, content with that answer, thanked Sven and turned with his supplies to go back upstairs.

"Aren't you forgetting something?" asked Sven.

"Of course," said Josh, shaking his head. Checking his notes, he grabbed the appropriate serum doses (Sven hoped) and abruptly exited the area, passing Adam on the way.

"Well..." Adam raised his eyebrows and extended his right arm as soon as Josh was clear of earshot. When Sven didn't answer, he asked, "What exactly did you find out? The serum? Is Charles Williams making any more progress than we are?"

Sven thought of the Cryonic chambers in his secret room. "Not really. I mean, he's trying, but he's hitting a lot of dead ends."

*He doesn't know what I am considering.*

"What do you know, Sven? Something is going on that you're not telling me. Your nephew visits and lasts for one day?"

"He had things to do." Sven shrugged.

"I don't buy it. What happened when Nathan came to visit? Look at me."

Sven stared at him straight in the face, crossing his arms. "I don't want to talk about it." Sven loosened his arms. "What do you need down here, anyway?"

"Here's my list." Adam snapped the paper open with a flick of the wrist and gave Sven the last page.

Sven went through the beakers, putting them in a tube rack.

"We are going to need to spruce up the security down here. A stronger door. It's important that no one gets down here. The serum is vital," said Adam.

"I agree." Sven checked the cooling systems, making sure they were at the right temperature. He thought about what he had read in the paperwork he stole. Charles was working on a special serum to bring people back from the dead. Still trying to wrap his head around it, one thought dwindled in his mind. Was he getting closer?

"You're quiet," Adam said. "What's on your mind?"

"Just thinking of the changes that need to be done down here. Changes that need to be done everywhere. We were on the right track, and everything's slipping." Sven leaned against a wall with no chairs available. "We had the virus in the water, and we worked on purifying it, but at that point, the mutants had contracted the infection. Then we found a serum, and it was getting better. We can't seem to make enough of it to cover the problem, and then there's the people misusing it. It could be the answer to the world, and they are using it for a high." Sven ran his hands through his thinning hair. "It's frustrating."

"I get it. It's frustrating for all of us. But we'll get there. Don't worry. I think this is a great place to keep the serum, and that is a place to start. You can't think of everything at once, but just take one step at a time, or you'll get exhausted."

"That's good advice. If it's all the same to you, I think I'm going to head back up to the rest of the facility. I have a lot to do today."

"Sure. I can gather the rest of them. I'll see you upstairs."

This time Sven walked the entire way.

— · —

# CHAPTER TWENTY-NINE

Sven was just heading to his last patient of the day when he heard Josh talking on the phone. As he got closer, he noticed Josh left the door cracked open in his office. Slowing down as he grew nearer, he listened with sharp ears.

"Yes, Mr. Williams, that would be great. I mean, Charles. Yes, I keep forgetting."

*What? He was friends with the creep? What was this all about?*

"Yes, I can stop by after your run. You know, I used to run track in my day. I could put on the running shoes and join you. You don't think I could keep up? Well, you may have a point, but the challenge is always there. I understand." There was a long pause. "Okay, I can meet you in an hour." Sven sped past as the conversation ended.

Josh's door slammed shut.

*If only I could be on that run, I might get valuable information. No wonder the man stayed so thin.*

An hour. *Following Josh is too risky.* He didn't wish to challenge that either. Then again, he was new, so he never got his own, but still...

"Dr. Olander..." one intern rushed to him down the hall, breaking his concentration. "I need your help. Hurry!" Sven ran down the hall and into a room where a patient was convulsing and jabbering nonsense. A girl that looked no older than seventeen was sweating, her long, red hair sticking to her face. Eye glowing a reddish brown, Sven didn't get too close. At least she was bound to the bed in the prevention of hurting herself.

"The serum. She's having withdrawals." Sven injected the spidomed with a medicine that would help with the side effects and placed it on her arm, a challenge when she was flopping about. "Help me, will you?" The intern rushed to hold her arm steady so he could place it securely enough for the medicine to absorb and do its job. Taking time to take effect, her thrashes slowed until she eventually fell asleep.

"Thank you."

"What's your name?" asked Sven.

"Greg."

"Well, Greg, you should have known what to do. This isn't the first addict here. You fill the spidomed, inject the medicine, and let it do its job. Do I make myself clear?"

"I'm sorry, I tried, but I couldn't get her to stay still long enough. You said so yourself, it was hard to do. I had to help you."

Sven glared at him. "Don't talk to your superiors like that. Do you understand me?" The man just nodded.

"I'm sorry I asked for your help." And he left the room.

Sven stood and watched the girl, dumbfounded by his own actions. The intern was right. Sven had no right to talk to him like that. He was just making sure he was keeping himself safe. His mind traveled back to when he was a new doctor at the institute, right after it opened. He wasn't as young as the man who had just left, but close. Graduated early in his class, he worked in a neighboring hospital before the great pandemic and the virus had spread to create mutants. He was the only doctor at Juniper Ridge who was old enough to remember what it was like before. A world without constant security and fear of what was going to happen right around the corner.

Looking at the woman lying in the bed, sedated almost enough to be unconscious, he could feel her trying to creep into his mind. "You listen to me, young lady. You need to stay off the drugs. If you lick this, we will use them to help the creatures that need it, humans and animals alike, and you can live in a world similar to where I used to live. No mutants, no danger other than people with dangerous actions from their own mind."

She stirred, pulling at the restraints with a moan in her sleep. Sven sang to her, a song that his mom sang to him when he was a boy. She relaxed, and in minutes she fell into a gentle sleep. A real sleep.

Satisfied that she was deep in slumber, Sven headed down to the bottom floor to see how Adam had progressed with the set-up. *We need to set up quickly so all the serum can be in one place.*

Glad for elevators, he made his way down, seeing fewer people as he got away from the main part of the building. The memories of going down into the basement, descending in the elevator, gave him a dropping feeling in his stomach.

Sven remembered heading down with Jesse, Adam, and Sam, so sure that they had found the way out. Tricked that day, Sam was an intern that was planted by Jill to spy on them and led them into the trap underneath the ground floor.

He heard someone in the new storage facility, and he wondered what Adam could be doing down there now, already getting so much done. Perhaps he had stocked the serum in the room already or was in the process. He could surely help him with that.

Peeking through the open door, he saw Josh's dress shirt and curly black hair.

"Josh, what are you doing down here?"

Josh jumped, flipping around with the look of a kid that gets caught getting cookies out of the jar.

"I needed more serum, and I didn't see any upstairs," he stammered. "For a patient, of course."

"Let me direct you upstairs, and I will show you where all the serum is, as soon as you tell me who this patient is." *Something is going on here. I am going to find out what it is.*

"Sure, it's Billy Mercer on the top floor."

"I thought you were more of an administrator than hands on, but I don't remember Billy Mercer," said Sven.

"Well, he got admitted when you were not here, and since the patient load is getting so large, I thought I would help with what I can."

Sven silently thought to himself, glad he didn't say it out loud. Gone with your wife while she was taking her last breath. It was possible that he didn't know Billy Mercer and followed Josh out the door, making sure it was closed tight behind him. When they did stock the room with serum, they would have to put extra cameras in, extra locks on the door, and do a retinal scan. It was much more effective than a fingerprint scan. Sven imagined the body parts that were once in the basement and pictured using one of someone's hands to get inside. He shook and tried to get the image out of his mind.

Josh reached a room where Sven could hear a quiet whining, and they both entered. A deformed tiger circled the cage, the ears eight in all lined up on the top of its head. Three eyes on each side of its head as well, in a total of six, gave it exceptional peripheral vision. Sven imagined what this animal was dealing with sensory overload. The noise in this facility must be extreme, and the view would be frightening, especially locked in a cage.

"This is Billy Mercer? But I thought…"

"Human name? I gave him the nickname, and it just stuck." Josh explained, "He reminds me of this kid in school. You couldn't sneak up on him for anything. It's like he had…"

"Eight ears and six eyes?" Sven smiled. "Brilliant. How has he been progressing so far?"

"He came in with poor lung function and blind in four of his eyes. I'm assuming the ones that aren't supposed to be there. But all his ears are fully functioning. His right side is a huge sore that won't heal, and now it is blistering instead of improving. I believe he's not getting enough of the serum to improve and is reverting back."

"I see." Sven saw the sadness in Josh's eyes and noticed the connection he had with Billy Mercer. "Let me look at the notes and see what I think the best plan of action is."

"That would be great." Josh and Sven left the room, Sven making a mental note to check on the patient. A lot of times more serum wouldn't help an animal like this. Slow and steady for animals was the way to go.

—·—

# CHAPTER THIRTY

Once Sven knew that Julia was doing better, and he had taken care of Josh's new favorite patient, he felt satisfied that it was time to address a different matter. He hadn't forgotten about Charles, keeping an eye on him to make sure he wasn't going to take all the serum and use it for his own plans. Yeah, and he wanted to make sure he could keep his promise. He missed Hannah so much it ached.

He called Nathan, lucky enough to catch him at work. In the police station, Sven requested privacy when talking to him, and to take the picture off of his phone. Who Nathan was talking to was no one's business. Curious, Nathan agreed and went into a private room, as promised, and got back to his uncle.

"Uncle Sven, I apologize. I shouldn't have left things the way things were. I know you're going through a lot. How are you doing?"

"I'm doing better, thank you," Sven lied. Having the picture gone was so much easier to fib, and he was glad he had taken it out of view. "I was wondering if you could do me a favor."

"Name it."

"Could you look into Charles Williams on your database? I wouldn't normally ask this, but it's important."

"You've piqued my curiosity. Why?" Sven could hear Nathan rustling papers.

"Well, I think he's breaking laws working against what we are doing here at Juniper. Doing it the official way would take longer. I just wondered if he has any plans of building something on the land that he currently purchased and if he has any paperwork and if he has any prior record. Sometimes people get into patterns."

Nathan chuckled. "So you do listen to me sometimes. Am I talking about work too much?"

"Nah. Just as a favor for me, could you do it? Make sure not to tell anyone? As a personal favor? I think Josh Freeman might be working with him as well."

"Just this once, considering I owe you. You can't make this a habit. Charles Williams and Josh Freeman?" Sven could hear Nathan writing down the names. "If they catch me doing this, I could get into serious trouble."

Sven got more comfortable at his desk at home. He leaned against the lamp, looking at a picture of his Hannah. "Just this once, and I would really appreciate it. I swear, when you come back to visit, it will be a much better one."

He could hear Nathan sigh on the other end of the phone. He hated to put his nephew in this position, but it would be so much easier for Nathan to do it, and he knew he could trust him not to tell anyone. Sven grabbed a dusty pen from a container on the edge of his desk, clicking the top so quickly he almost broke it.

"Okay," Nathan agreed, and Sven threw the pen back in its holder, holding in the urge to jump up and down with glee. Well, he could do something like that. Nathan couldn't see him.

"Are you sure this is such a good idea? Maybe it is a better idea to go through the proper channels?"

"I am asking you. You could say no..." Sven groaned, crossing his fingers. Please say yes. He opened the top drawer of his desk and pulled out a Milky Way. Undoing the wrapper, he put the whole mini candy bar in his mouth.

"You're eating chocolate, aren't you?" asked Nathan.

"Yes. So?" He spoke with his mouth full, muffling his voice.

"Okay, I'll do it," chuckled Nathan. "Just give me some time."

"The faster the better."

"I'll talk to you when I'm done. You want me to be thorough, right?"

"Of course," said Sven with a sigh. "Thanks, kid. I appreciate it."

Sven hung up and stood to stretch, throwing the candy bar wrapper in the garbage. There was no way he was just going to sit here and wait. It was time to take action, and soon. Considering Charles' threat, maybe it was time to ask for more help from the people that he could trust most. Calling Jesse and Adam, he made plans to gather together in the morning. Putting it off wasn't an option, although he couldn't let them know anything about the deal that he was contemplating.

*What am I going to tell them?*

The thought reverberated through his mind until, finally, he drifted off to sleep.

# CHAPTER THIRTY-ONE

The sun shone through the trees, the air void of smog and darkness. Birds chirped; the scent of wildflowers covered the countryside. A stream gurgled nearby and there was the sound of children's laughter with the squeaking of a swing set.

Kimberly's blonde curls flew in the wind as she pumped her legs, her round cheeks red that matched the bow in her hair. The little girl next to her was saying, "higher and higher," and Kimberly kept laughing.

"I win, I win!" Kimberly yelled to the little girl after reaching the highest part of the tree, slowing down to jump off the swing and run off. "You can't catch me!" With a perfect dismount, the dirt clouded under her feet before she jetted off in a sprint.

"You better believe I can, but I want to swing," laughed the second girl.

Kimberly spotted white butterflies. She chased after them to dance with.

The sky turned dark as the smog rolled in to hide the sun and a wind whistled through the trees. Kimberly ran back to the swing set, but it wasn't there and the other little girl was gone. Kimberly looked up in confusion until the smog formed a hand that grabbed her by the hair and pulled her into the sky. She screamed as the wind and rain swirled all around her.

Thrown back into the now dark and rainy woods, Kimberly dropped in the mud with a thud. Everything enveloped in a dark cloud of smog, her hair was wet and in disarray, sticking to the side of her face. Chiffon from her tattered dress hung from her. The swing set was gone, as well as the other child. Kimberly cried.

Until she heard a growling. Eyes growing wide, she stayed as silent as she could, clinching onto the mud on the ground as if it could save her.

Charles woke up drenched in sweat. Catching his breath, he checked the time. Three A.M.

"What a nightmare," he muttered, putting on a robe to thwart the chill that entered the room. After going to the bathroom and splashing some cold water on his face, he headed to the cryogenic chambers below.

Placing his hand on her chamber, Charles bowed his head. "Oh, Kimberly, I am so sorry for what happened to you. You were just playing up in the trees like a normal kid should. You shouldn't have fallen. I miss you terribly." His stomach clinched. He thought of his dream, and tears fell. "Is that where you are right now? Somewhere safe?"

He never believed in an afterlife. Now he wondered if there was some truth in it. Am I pulling you out of heaven to bring you back here just to be with me? Is that what you were trying to tell me? If so, this could be one of the most selfish things I have ever done.

With clenched fists, he let go and exhaled the breath he was holding. "Sweetheart, I can't do that to you." Hands shaking, he placed his right one on the plug of the chamber and let out short, rapid breaths. His forehead tensed.

"No." Charles pulled his hand back. "What am I doing? It was just some stupid dream. I love you Kimberly, and I'll see you soon." He scrunched down until he was sitting next to his daughter and fell asleep.

# Chapter Thirty-Two

Sven woke from sleeping nine hours straight, the most that he had slept in years. He stretched, hanging his legs over the side of the bed. He paused, gripping the edge of the mattress, narrowing his eyes and looking around. A clunking reverberated up the stairs.

Opening the drawer of his nightstand, he pulled out the strongest tranquilizer gun available that he always kept ready to go. Standing up, he paused. There was silence, then another noise underneath him. He walked on the balls of his feet, hoping the creaking of the floor wouldn't give him away.

Once he made it to the top of the stairs, he could smell the coffee. Mutants didn't stop to make coffee, and neither did intruders. He lowered his weapon when he saw a figure come out of the shadows.

"Hey, Sven!" Sven jumped, lifting up the tranquilizer gun, the dart flying right past Adam's head and landing in the wall behind him.

Adam lifted up his hands in surrender. "It's me, Sven, and Jesse. We come in peace."

Sven put his hand to his chest. "You can't surprise an old man like that. What are you two doing here?" Sven then felt the breeze as he was only in his boxer shorts, his face flushing. Jesse came into view with a coffeepot.

"Whoa," Jesse said, staring at the dart in the wall. "I knew we were supposed to meet you here this morning. We thought we would surprise you with breakfast."

"Well," said Sven, "as long as there's more than that pot of coffee." The scent of sausage and biscuits invaded his nostrils. "I'm just going to put some pants on, and I will be down. I would say sorry for almost tranquilizing you, but you had it coming, sneaking up on me like that." He grumbled on the way to the bathroom, but he couldn't say much. He was starving.

After going to the bathroom and splashing some cold water on his face, he blotted it dry. What a life. He thought of everything that had transpired in the last couple of weeks. Losing Hannah, the cryonics facility, Charles, work, arguing with Nathan. What would Hannah say to all of this? What would she say once she comes back? Looking in the mirror, he swore he saw her standing behind him, watching him without saying a word. Hope filled his heart, and he caught his breath. Flipping around, she wasn't there.

His stomach grumbled again, and he followed his nose to the kitchen. Jesse had a steaming pile of gravy and a mound of biscuits. Sven sat at the table.

"We have a lot to talk about," said Adam, sipping on his coffee and sprinkling pepper on his breakfast. "It sounds like you've been holding out on us. We can't help you if we don't know what you're thinking."

"Yeah, Sven. What have you been keeping from us?" asked Jesse. Sven stayed silent, sifting through all that had been happening, to decide what exactly he was going to tell them. "Don't tell us it's nothing. I don't think your car was wrecked because you happened to be attacked by a mutant. You're more careful than that."

"Well...it did happen. A mutant attacked me." He tore apart his biscuit, pouring gravy over it. "You know they are getting worse with the shortage and all, and people aren't as careful with that false sense of security that we are holding the cure in our hands."

"But you are," said Adam. "It doesn't make sense."

"Less security in general. Some of the fences aren't even properly maintained." He took a healthy bite of breakfast, letting the spices and sausage linger in his mouth. "That isn't my fault. It could have happened to any of us. I wonder...what do you two know about Josh?" Sven asked.

"Josh is Daniel's brother. He can't be that bad," said Adam.

"And Jill is his daughter, and we all know how well that all turned out. I don't know if I buy his story of his capture. I'm sure someone could have vouched for him. And he's...weird." Sven thought of how he went down to the lab and almost forgot the serum.

"Yeah, he's a little off," said Jesse. "So?"

"No, it's something else," said Sven. "He keeps his distance around the patients, like he hasn't been around a lot of mutants and people thought he was against curing the mutants? Maybe he was. Nathan is looking into him." Pointing his finger at them, he said, "You two are to make sure no one knows about Nathan helping us out."

"It could be a coincidence," said Adam, "but I don't know. All of that's strange."

"I just asked Nathan, so I don't have any information yet," he said between bites. He was just so hungry. The recent events had taken a lot out of him. Sven watched Jesse and noted the steadiness of his footing, the color of his cheeks, and his once bloodshot eyes clear. The wonders of modern medicine had him healed almost to normal in five days. If it wasn't for the scar of deep, pink ridges on his left cheek, no one would ever know of the attack.

"And how are you since you've been out of the hospital, Jesse?"

"I feel great." Jesse put his hand on Sven's shoulder, a grin lighting up his face. "Jennifer is coming over for dinner. I have a date."

*Maybe it's more than just modern medicine?* Sven smiled as he thought of the young nurse.

"So, what are you going to cook?" asked Adam. "If I were you, I would…"

Sven interrupted. "Oh, no, don't ask the man that brings peanut butter and bologna sandwiches to work. We will discuss this later. I know a thing or two about cooking."

Adam lifted his hands in surrender, retreating from the conversation.

"How is the family, Adam?" asked Sven. *Sven prayed they were all doing well. He was having enough problems for all of them. I have to catch up with them and connect with them. Heaven only knows how long I am going to be here.*

"They're fine. Henry is walking, and Camille is into everything from painting to karate. Sometimes I wish they could stay little forever."

Sven asked about his wife, Rachel.

"She is selling some paintings. We'll see where it goes, but it could be the beginning of a career."

"I've got to get over there sometime and see them," said Sven. "The family and the paintings."

"Yeah, you're welcome anytime. We should have a get together or maybe you could come over for dinner sometime. We're having a party for Camille's karate. She graduated with a blue belt. I would love to be there, but no way am I jeopardizing all of this blowing up in our faces. I won't be a mutant again." Adam stared at the wall as he spoke. "I feel bad. She's putting her heart and soul into this. I've never seen her so excited."

"You should go," said Sven.

"Hey, we'll go with you," agreed Jesse.

"I will make it up to her." Adam rubbed his forehead and played with his food on his plate. "As long as she doesn't hate me. I don't want to be one of those dads."

"You'll never be one of those dads," said Jesse.

The phone rang, and Sven noticed it was Nathan.

Wanting some privacy, he let the men know he would be right back, and went into the living room, sitting in his recliner and kicking his legs back. Nathan's face showed up on his wrist.

"I'm calling because I found nothing on the name you gave me. Are you alone?" asked Nathan, and Sven saw him clicking on the keys on the computer.

"Yes, just me," confirmed Sven.

"I can't find anything on Josh at all. Just that he's related to Daniel Freeman and Jill Freeman. The last I see of him on the internet is Josh Freeman, listed in Daniel's obituary. He's lived nowhere, no wife, no kids, no job...I looked into everything."

"Okay," said Sven. What was he doing before the records started on the computer? He had to have more history with his position at Juniper Ridge.

"Sorry I couldn't be more helpful," said Nathan. "I hope that makes you feel better about him."

"You've been a big help. Thank you so much." Sven gave him a smile. "I love you. I hope you know that."

"I love you, too. That's why I worry about you." Nathan sighed. "I really should get going. Talk to you later?"

"Yeah, okay," said Sven. "Thank you."

In the other room Sven could hear the others cleaning up, and thought of how lucky he was to have those two. Reclining in his chair, he thought of all the research, the stress, the sneaking around that he had been doing, and he was done. It was time to do something for good.

But could he side with Charles? Could Charles bring Hannah back? He didn't want to close that door, but he couldn't wait all his life for it to open, either. When the time came, he better hold up his part of the bargain. Sven could still help plan something as long as it's obvious he's not a part of it.

*I'm tired of waiting. For Charles to use all the serum. For Hannah to come back. Selfish or not, I'm done.*

Sven flipped up the recliner, stood straight and tall before treading into the kitchen. "We need to gather everyone," declared Sven, entering the kitchen. "That will prove who's really for us, and who's not. We should have a meeting at Juniper Ridge. The more on our side, the better." *And it will take attention off of me. We can still fight Charles, and maybe, by some miracle, I can get her back. She has to come back to me.*

"That's a good idea," said Adam, putting down his dish drying towel, "and entirely legal at that."

"We can take care of this," agreed Jesse. "I need to play my part in it, too." Jesse shoved his thumb toward his chest. "My turn to take care of business."

"We need a plan and people to back us up. I would say take it straight to the source," said Sven.

Both of the other men nodded in agreement. "That's right," said Jesse.

"Take it straight to the tree," said Adam.

# CHAPTER THIRTY-THREE

"Sven, just the man I wanted to see," said Josh, coming out of Julia's room. Sven stopped from rushing down the hall on his way to the meeting that he was planning, the thought of Julia stopping him in his tracks.

"Is she okay?" he asked, pointing to her door.

Josh grinned. "She is doing remarkably well. If things keep going the way they are, we should discharge her and integrate her back into society. We already have a few doctors that have volunteered to watch out for her and give her a home until she gets settled."

"That's great!" *Things are finally looking my way. If we can cure Julia, think of all the good we can do for the other patients.*

"Of course, she will need her proper doses for a while after, a little at a time, until fully recovered."

"Of course." *More serum. That's always the issue, isn't it?* Knowing the big decision was creeping up, his stomach turned sour. "If you will excuse me, sir, I have somewhere to be."

"Yes, we will discuss this more as she improves. Nice work, doctor." Josh reached out to shake his hand.

"Thank you." Sven continued down the hall, wondering if he imagined the conversation. It seemed all too good to be true, and he told himself not to get his hopes up.

Was it going to come down to Julia or Hannah? The mutants or his wife?

Jesse broke his train of thought as he called to him down the hallway. Sven nodded as Jesse patted him on the back. With a deep breath, he asked, "Are you ready?"

Sven nodded before they entered the conference room as the scientists were filing in. Laughter and conversation filled the room, and Sven wondered how many people actually showed up. He wasn't expecting such a big turnout, but he was glad. He knew he could use all the help he could get with this monumental task. His stomach was alive with nerves, and he was hoping could keep down his breakfast. All eyes turned to him, knowing he was the one that called the meeting. The full room warmed him and made him clammy and sweaty. His ears rang as claustrophobia set in. Taking deep breaths, he reached the podium on one end of the room.

"Are you okay?" asked Adam, standing very near Sven. *Why would he do that? I need my space.* Sven nodded, but his head was the only thing that moved. The rest of him was completely still, along with the rest of the room. Everyone had taken their seats and waited to see what the news was.

All eyes were on him. "Thank you all for coming. I know we haven't had a meeting like this in some time, and I think you would all like to know what is happening, and what we can do to stop it. I appreciate everything that we all do here, trying to implement the cure the best that we know how. Return the world to what it once was. We've come upon some roadblocks and I say that we take care of those once and for all!"

"What are we going to do?" asked a young lady, standing up near the middle of the room. "I know that people are breaking in. Are we going to beef up security?"

"It's more than just a security problem. There may be a new threat in town. Charles Williams just bought property, and it includes the tree of life." Everyone talked at once, some stood up in a fury.

"He can't do that."

"Is that legal?"

"Doesn't he care? He could ruin everything."

"Kill the bastard."

"Now hold on." Sven said, raising his hands in the air, yelling, "stop now! We can work together. He can't be against all of us. We need to make a plan."

"Sven," he heard from the back of the room. Josh stood up, walking toward the front with wide strides. "Can I have a word with you?"

"Of course." Josh glanced at the group of people watching him with intense eyes.

"Privately." Sven swore he saw the wind come out of every-one's sails. "In the hall."

Adam gave a questioning look at Sven. "I'll be all right," Sven assured him. "Two minutes," he said. "We have already wasted enough time. I will be right back," he announced to the rest of the crowd.

Sven was glad to be out of the room filled with people, and could breathe easier in the hallway. "What?"

"You can't go against him."

"I knew you would say that." Sven took two steps back from Josh. "I knew you were on his side."

"What? His side?" Josh took a step back and shook his head. "That wasn't what I said. It's not safe."

"You don't even know me."

"But my brother did, and even though we weren't on the best of speaking terms all the time, I know what this place meant to him, and I know what it means to you. I can see it when you work with your patients. Charles Williams is dangerous. He has a lot of power and I don't want to see you get hurt."

"I can't get hurt any more than I already am," said Sven, thinking of his Hannah. "So I don't care. I'm going to do it either way, and there's nothing you can do to stop me."

"Okay, so I am going with you." Sven paused, surprised. Was there a piece of Daniel in Josh? Maybe he wasn't the bad man that Sven thought, but then he remembered Sam and how he deceived them all, leading Adam, Jesse, and himself underneath the building with the ruins of the mutants. His trust was thinning.

"You can't go with me. I don't even know you." Sven's eyes narrowed. "But we could use all the help we can get. My question is, what do you mean, dangerous? What do you know I don't know?"

"He has many people that work underneath him, and some of them aren't on the straight and narrow like he tries to portray. That's all I'm saying," said Josh, holding up his hands in surrender. "I try to do my homework. Research is kind of my thing, but I don't use computers. I observe and ask questions. And I have another suggestion." Josh raised his eyebrows, then looked beside Sven, unable to meet his eyes.

"We should make this quick. There are people waiting."

"Jill should help. This would be her last chance to do something good before she goes off to prison to finish her sentence. They're saying she's almost well enough to leave here."

"No!" Sven stepped further away from him, flying around his arms. "She's a crook, not to mention mentally unstable. She is against us, not with us, and it has always been that way. Nothing has changed." Sven went to open the door of the conference room again, not even looking at Josh. Absolutely not with Jill, but could he really trust Josh? He needed help if he was to take down Charles, and it sounded like Josh knew about the man, or at least about his associates. *Don't let this bite me in the ass.*

"Not Jill," he said again, about ready to open the door. "She's a prisoner and it would be against her sentence to leave Juniper Ridge to any other location than jail. Come in, and let's see what we can all do together."

The boardroom was a bustle of activity. Adam and Jesse were right by Sven's side as he returned, asking questions about what went on in the hall. Sven simply acknowledged that Josh was going to assist, but left out the part about Charles being dangerous. Surely, they must all know that by now.

A protest, a rally, and with all of them there, there was no way that Charles could continue building on the land. Destruction of the tree of life would be at a halt. Time was of the essence. Two days, and they would storm the construction going on. Sven would make sure they would create a ring around the tree to make sure of its safety. He wondered if Charles harmed the protective dome since he had been out there. If so, any mutant could harm the precious tree.

He wondered how long the serum would work after Hannah had passed away. Or did Charles even find a cure? If he had, was he destroying the chances of ever bringing her back?

He would make sure to talk to Charles, just to see if he had a cure. But what if he did? What would he do then? His head hurt and he looked out over all the eager faces of the scientists trying to help. Was he being a hypocrite standing in front of all of them to make a difference?

The question that pulsed at his brain was: What would Hannah think?

The men and women were chanting Sven's name, ready to fight for the cause. They made a plan to gather weapons, have a meeting place, and travel together. Sven would get a hold of the MCS. Surely they would be on their side. They were as interested as anyone to cure the mutants, risking their lives every day to keep society safe.

The back door opened and closed with a bang. The room became silent as Josh walked up to the podium and shook Sven's hand. "It's about time we did something about this. I never liked that man one bit." The room was an eruption of clapping and hollering.

They all had work to do.

Sven exited the room last after sitting in a conference room chair, taking a deep breath. This was finally it. It was time to take care of this once and for all. He had to make sure, and making sure no one was in the room, tapped on his watch and called Charles.

"Sven, hello," said Charles. "What a surprise. What can I do for you?" Smiling and petting his dog, he appeared to be in front of a fireplace.

"We made a deal," said Sven. "It's time for you to hold up your end of the bargain."

"We made a deal that you wouldn't sabotage my company while I am working on a cure to bring your wife back. More than a cure for mutants, a cure for death. A drug above all drugs that will cure anything. As far as I know, you haven't done anything against your end of the bargain. If you are asking about progress, I am still working on it."

"And how is that going?" asked Sven. "Have you found a cure?"

"Perhaps, but I will have to test it out. It will take a significant amount of serum to bring someone back from the dead, but I believe it is possible."

"Why should I believe you?"

"It's up to you, but remember our conversation." His Hannah would be back. Closing his eyes, he could smell her strawberry lotion she smothered on her hands every night before bed, the way she looked over his shoulder as he read, her soft kiss in the morning. But he would have to take so much serum. The mutants would grow in number again to where they were before, addicts or not. They wouldn't be able to replenish the serum fast enough and they would be back to square one in days. Then they would be dealing with addicts and mutants. At least the addicts wouldn't have any temptation. There wouldn't be serum to steal. "Are you sure this will work?"

"I'm sure. Where do you want to meet so I can hold up my end of the bargain?"

"Two days," said Sven. "The tree of life. Seven in the morning."

"Fine," said Charles. "I will meet you then."

"Two days," muttered Sven after he got off the phone. "I have two days to choose." He shook as he rose from his chair and wished Hannah was there for such a decision. But this time, she was the decision.

Hannah or the world?

$-\cdot-$

# CHAPTER THIRTY-FOUR

The air was crisper than normal that night, and the smell of pine trees played with Sven's nose as he climbed up the hill. After ten minutes of walking, he looked back, and he could still see his car. He knew he was almost there. Not that much longer.

The mist of the smog enveloped him, mixed with fog and dew on the grass. Mud clung to his shoes that made a sticking sound, making his feet heavier with each step. Was it really the mud, or the thoughts that plagued his mind? *I have to see Luke. I haven't been up here in so long.*

The metal fence around the tombstone was small and rusty, hardly able to keep mutants from messing with the burial site. But yet, nothing touched the sacred ground. There was no gate, but just an opening to one side. Sven shook his head at the overgrown grass and coppery smell of the earth, disappointed in himself for not coming out and taking care of things. He knew he had a good reason, aside from the fact that this was a very dangerous place to be. Back when Lucas was buried there, there was no forbidden zone. He bent down to pull the overgrown grass around his tombstone, which made the tombstone appear larger.

"Lucas, I know I haven't been up here in a long time." Sven squatted down to the grave, as if the child could hear him better from a lower point of view. "I'm sorry for that." He pictured the blonde, brown-eyed five-year-old playing with his G.I. Joe's throughout the house. Sven couldn't remember how many times he stepped on those things, and the thought made him laugh, and cry a little. "I should have died in that accident," he told him. "The only son I ever had, gone in an instant. I loved you so much. I loved you more than my life."

He pictured another headstone next to Lucas'. A larger grave, with the name "Hannah Olander" next to it. It would have flowers in the corners. Hannah loved her flowers. Maybe, perhaps, she should be out here, too, instead of that Cryonic building down on 35th and Main in a tank keeping her body alive. Was she really there at all?

Maybe she should, and he should as well. He pictured a gravestone for two, Hannah Olander and Sven Olander. He placed his hand on the soil where it would be embedded and then stretched out on the dirt where the grass struggled to grow. To be six feet under. All the problems and worries behind him, the pain and the suffering.

Maybe I should be dead, too. Then we would all be together. Closing his eyes, he took in the rich smell of the earth and the pine trees in the distance. Envisioning being there forever, the threat of Charles coming after him didn't scare him, but he wished it. Peace forever.

Taking a deep breath, he sat up and brushed himself off. No, that would be defeat and he doesn't take defeat. Sven knew his crucial role was to save the world. He couldn't save Lucas, but he can save Hannah. Failure is not an option.

No, no, unacceptable. That would be throwing away everything, all his hopes and dreams, and he would be all alone. Maybe someday all three of them would be together again, and things would be different. For now, he had to have Hannah back. Lucas couldn't have her yet.

He tried to fill his mind with memories, the G.I. Joe's, playing puppets, and reading him a story at bedtime. Lucas' last day on earth flashed through his mind, intruding on his happy times.

Sven took the day off of work to drive young Lucas to his first day of kindergarten. He was going at the regular speed, and the car in front of him just stopped in one second. There was nothing he could do. The airbags went off, and they were both taken to the nearest hospital. Sven was out in a week with a broken leg.

Lucas didn't get to come home.

"I'm sorry, son," Sven said to the grave. "I'm not ready to give up on your mom." He placed the artificial flowers on his grave, and next to his name placed three G.I. Joes.

# CHAPTER THIRTY-FIVE

I t was seven in the morning, and Sven was shaking. *What am I going to do? I have to see proof of the cure with my own eyes.* He knew the rest of the group was gathering at eight, knowing that's when Charles began his daily construction, the site getting closer and closer to the tree. Now the group against Charles were in a meeting to make sure they were all on the same page. Sven had made up an excuse, some last-minute details to take care of, and made sure Adam knew to tell the others that he was meeting them at the tree of life.

The tree of decision.

The tree of choices.

The tree of miracles.

The walk to the tree wasn't far from the parking area. A half an hour for him, probably shorter for the average man. It gave him time to think and reflect. It was an unusually sunny day, but he knew the forecast called for showers and maybe even a thunderstorm. Once he stepped into the woods, the atmosphere darkened from the shadowing trees. Carefully, he made sure he knew where he was going, checking the coordinates on his watch. He pictured the woods on a dark, dreary night and wondered what it would be like if he were Adam when he transformed into a mutant. Poor Adam. That must have been terrifying. His palms sweated profusely.

With each step, he made sure he had a weapon handy: a knife sheathed on his belt to his left and a tranquilizer gun gripped tightly in his right hand.

He found the tree in the distance, where the others parted and it stood out all on its own. Sven could hear the tree frogs reminding him of a younger Sven. Even using the tree frogs as a serum, they always leave a few at the site, as if the magic of the forest will shine through the remedy and give not only medicinal elements, but magical ones. Sven wasn't sure how he felt about all that.

Opening the gate and going in, he leaned against the tree. Once again, he was a child going out to the forest to gather frogs. He remembered playing with them as a boy, not knowing the importance that they would have in the future. Playing freely in the woods is something that children haven't been able to do in a long time, unless they were in areas surrounded by fences and guards. MCS everywhere.

Sven remembered when holidays came around and the house filled with family. Laughter and children's feet running through the house, no matter how many times Mom and Dad told them all to slow down. The youngest of eight brothers and sisters made for a full house, but he never imagined the day he would be the last one living. He existed for Hannah.

And now she is gone.

There was the rest of the world to think about, and his dear friends he had made along the way. They loved him and wanted what was best for him.

He heard footsteps, or what he thought were footsteps, when he turned around to a creature that he had never seen before. Towering over Sven with red googly eyes and rancid breath, it stood on its two legs like a human. The skin was brown and coarse, blending well into the forest, antlers perched between two small, doe-like ears. He could smell it from a distance from the creature's putrid overall odor. Its legs were the size of ancient tree trunks with flat, furry feet and round toes. A rotund torso made it hard for the creature to move quickly, the thin, under-developed arms appeared as if they were trying to extend farther than the two feet they were allowed. Sven raised his tranquilizer gun, small enough to be compact and carry anywhere. But there was no need. The creature collapsed right in front of him, right after the boom of a shotgun.

Sven's heart raced. Who could have killed the mutant? His eyes jumped from area to area as he sunk to a crouched position, ready to strike. Then he heard a familiar voice.

"It's just me." Charles stepped out of the trees, a smoking pistol in his hand that he put away in a holster. "You're welcome. Can't be too careful these days." Sven watched the mutant, but with no movement at all, he assumed it was dead. At least Sven had the time to reflect before he made any kind of decision about the deal. Charles wouldn't know for sure that Sven had anything to do with the fight. If Charles had something he wanted that desperately, he just might turn the tables...he wouldn't fight against his friends. He was sure his hair was getting grayer as he stood there.

"Are you ready for our discussion?" asked Charles, pulling out a vial one inch tall from his pocket. "I am holding in my hand the most concentrated serum for mutations EVER."

Sven reached out his hand, but Charles pulled the vial far away from him. "All in good time. You have to realize what this means. Handing you this vial is an agreement between you and I, and in this is a concentration of 1000 doses of the serum." Charles clinched the vial tight. "One drop of this might cure a mutant, but this vial can bring someone back." Charles' eyes widened and brightened.

"This is all because of you, Sven, and I just wanted you to know how grateful I am."

Sven shook his head, trying to remember anything he could have done to help him.

"Those notes you wrote on the paperwork you found." Charles' eyes brightened, and he shook his index finger in Sven's direction. "You are a smart one. Those notes helped with problems we were running into."

Sven thought of the world covered in mutants, the threat returning. He pictured Jesse in the road, bleeding as Sven put pressure on the wound so he wouldn't lose his friend. He remembered the accident with the bobcat-like mutant and all the people that were injured. Feeling Hannah's hand on his shoulder, he closed his eyes. She wouldn't want him to work with someone like Charles or Hannah's existence to be the reason for suffering and the chance of a better world. He will see her again someday, just not today.

"No," Sven murmured.

"What?" Charles leaned in. "I thought we had an agreement. I don't understand. Don't you want her back?"

Sven's breath caught in his throat. Charles had no idea how much he wanted her back.

"Not at this cost. I won't do that to her and I won't do it to humanity. No," Sven said, louder with more force. Sven's body tensed up, but he also felt a sense of relief, as if someone had lifted a weight off him. "The people that are still here are the ones that need to be saved. The fate of humanity is within all of us, and now is the time to take responsibility. It's time for me to stop being so damn selfish."

"Fine, I even brought my proof." A child walked through the trees, whom he assumed was Kimberly.

At first, Sven thought from a distance she was dirty from running through the woods, but as he got closer, he saw the open sores that took over her body that oozed pus. The left eye dripped blood like she was crying red, leaving a trail down her cheek. She smelled of decay and death. Her blonde hair, littered with leaves and branches, hung past her waist like old moss. She walked with an uneven gait, dragging one foot behind her.

"Come to Daddy," Charles said, crouched down with outstretched arms.

Kimberly didn't speak as she stared straight ahead. When she reached Charles, he scooped her up in his arms and held her.

Sven watched, not moving, and was instantly glad that he didn't take Charles up on his offer. Kimberly didn't talk, crack a smile, or show any awareness of the world around her. It was as if she was sleeping with her eyes open, possessed or controlled by something else. A shell of what she once was.

"I'm sorry it wasn't a success," said Sven to Charles, and he meant it. "I thought you were going to try it on the other child first."

Charles looked up and shook his head. "It's a total success. She's alive. I love you, Kimberly," he whispered in her ear. "There wasn't enough to experiment with. It takes too much."

"She's not the same." Sven instantly wished he could take it back. Charles clutched onto what was once his little girl, glaring at Sven.

"What do you expect? These things take time. She will heal. She just came back from the dead!" He stopped himself, then stroked Kimberly's hair. "I'm sorry, baby. Daddy didn't mean to raise his voice."

A loud crash echoed through the forest like a continuous breaking of tree limbs through the trees. Charles and Sven both turned to see machines coming at them, the scientists behind the wheels. Charles made a mad rush for cover so he wouldn't get run over, clinching onto his daughter. Sven stood next to the tree while they surrounded it.

Adam looked down at Sven from the controls, eyes wide and mouth agape, narrowing his brows in confusion. "You can't destroy the tree," he spoke to Charles, but his gaze never left Sven. "We're all here to make sure that doesn't happen."

"That's right!" interjected Jesse, pulling up from another machine.

"I don't want to destroy the tree." Charles stood in front of Adam's machine, hands raised in the air. "It's to make serum, like it always has. Cure the mutants so we can live in safety."

*He's lying!* Yelled in Sven's brain, but it couldn't reach his lips. He doesn't want to use the serum to cure mutants at all.

"Why don't I believe you?" asked Jesse.

"None of us believe you," said another scientist, her voice shrill through the forest.

"Look, I have the miracle cure." Charles held up the vial, his grip unwavering, still clinging to Kimberly. "It's the serum, concentrated."

"Why?" asked Jesse.

"To bring back someone from the dead! Concentrated ingredients of the frog DNA are in here. It's a miracle. Look at my little girl. She's living proof it works." Adam and Jesse both cast their attention on Kimberly. Adam's face softened while Jesse's hardened.

"Do you realize you are destroying the entire civilization as we know it manufacturing that?" pipped in one scientist.

Cop cars rolled in the clearing around the tree, similar in build like the MCS. They had to be strong against the mutants and fast. Uniformed officers got out of their vehicles, weapons at the ready. They wore safety clothing similar to MCS, but not as extensive. Three cars down, Sven recognized the officer.

Josh.

*No wonder he couldn't find any information in his history. It is likely that they wiped it clean for security reasons. Undercover. Sneaky.*

The sound of more machinery from the forest made Sven's stomach churn. All the trees that took years to grow. He understood the necessity, but didn't mean he had to like it. Machines twice as big as the Juniper Ridge scientists' surrounded them. Charles' men surrounded the area, sneaking into spots between the Juniper Ridge.

"What's going on here?" asked one guy, scratching his mustache, taken aback by Kimberly. "I thought we were supposed to get some headway done. Boss, what's the plan? Who are these people?"

"Just a misunderstanding," said Charles, putting Kimberly down but keeping a death grip on her hand. "They are all leaving."

"We aren't going anywhere," Adam said, the others joining in. One of the Juniper Ridge machines moved full force, ramming into one of Charles' men hard enough to jar him, falling out of the machine. Another one ran into Adam.

Machines were breaking all around them, people leaping out of them, and they came out swinging.

Staring at the vial, he went to grab it, but Charles pulled it out of reach. The vial that could help a thousand mutants? If he was being truthful, that vial was worth its weight in gold. "You said no to our deal, so this is no longer yours to take."

Josh walked toward Charles, a gun pointed at him as he yelled, "Put your hands up! Charles Williams, you are under arrest."

Another uniformed officer was right beside him. Sven noted Josh fully equipped in a cop uniform. He appeared more comfortable and sure of himself.

Charles scowled at Josh. "A cop, I should have known." Charles shook his head. "That story about always being the black sheep of the family..." He refused to let go of Kimberly's hand, but he lifted his left one in surrender after slipping the vial into his pants pocket. When he didn't get a reply, he said, "I don't have any weapons. What are the charges?"

"You purchased this land illegally and employees at Williams Pharmaceutical are dealing serum, or whatever your drug dealers are telling people."

Sven raised his eyebrows, remembering the vial that they found on the addicts matching the vial they found at his facility.

"I purchased this land legally, and I know nothing about the selling of serum except through the proper channels." Charles clenched his jaw. "Actual serum. If anything else is going on, I did not know it was happening."

"You can tell it to the judge."

Sven heard something rustling in the fallen leaves. At first he thought it was the weather, but then he heard the scream of the second officer as he bent down to grip his ankle. "What the hell?" A neon yellow snake wrapped around his leg, where normally one head was four, and all four forked tongues lashed out, biting him. Wherever the creature touched, his skin left a sticky residue. He gripped it to pull it off, but it just clung and kept squeezing.

Kimberly reached out to grab the creature, clasping it in her claws, puncturing it as it bled. She peeled it off the stunned officer like she was ripping off a band-aid.

The officer yelled, and Kimberly grasped his leg, her claws digging into the officer.

Sven flipped out his tranquilizer gun, and the dart hit her shoulder at a close enough range to fall before Charles caught her. Charles gently placed her behind the tree, his eyes drooping, narrowing as he jutted out his bottom lip. Jaw protruding before standing in one fluid motion, flipping around, and punched Sven square in the jaw.

Sven staggered backward before regaining his balance, rubbing his jaw with his right hand, his face beginning to swell.

The tranquilizer gun wasn't enough for Kimberly, who opened her eyes wide and pulled the dart out without even looking at it.

Sven's breath caught in his throat. *Tranquilizer darts don't work on her?* His face hurt with every slight movement.

"Stop!" warned Josh to Charles, keeping one eye on his partner, who was grasping his leg in pain on the ground and Charles, fists balled up in front of his face, legs spread, and turning in all directions ready to punch the next person who got near his daughter.

"No, don't hurt her," said Charles, moving in front of her. "I won't allow it. She pulled the mutant off, trying to help. What happened to the cop was an accident."

Two MCS vehicles drove through the only opening left in the trees, which was a tight fit. A tall, brawny woman jumped out of the driver's side, paralyzer gun at the ready. Her pixie black hair and dark eyes stayed with Kimberly. "Get away from the mutant!" she yelled. "I have her." Her partner was out of the truck in seconds, on the other side of her as backup. Other MCS moved in closer to the girl.

Kimberly's eyes bled tears that fell on her floral dress. She latched on to her father's hand with a death grip, extended nails elongated from the nail beds.

Charles grimaced as the fingernails punctured his wrists. The metallic smell of blood filled the air. The other officer moved to grab Kimberly, when Charles said, "Don't touch her or I will kill you." Blood dripped from his wrists in a steady rhythm. His focus continued on Kimberly.

The paralyzer gun cast a ray that struck Kimberly's shoulder from the backside Charles couldn't protect her from. Kimberly remained frozen, tears and all.

"I'll protect you, baby," he cooed to her, reaching into the inner part of his leg and pulling out a knife in front of him, his grasp tight, his hands shaking. Widening his stance, he moved his head from one side to the other. "Paralyzer guns are effective for ten minutes, so if you're going to get us, you better do it fast."

One of the burly men running the dump truck spoke up, jumping out of the truck to join Charles. "I'm with you, sir. This man is brilliant. You're all just jealous."

A fight engulfed the construction site. A Juniper Ridge scientist shot a tranquilizer arrow at the man from a distance, and he fell instantly, the dirt floor clouding of dust around him. Another scientist threw a spidomed at a construction worker and they fell out of the excavator. Men and women were fighting with fists, weapons, and anything else they could find. Most of the MCS stayed out of the fights, but continued to watch for mutants, keeping their pledge to provide safety for humans.

Three young MCS made their way through the crowd, their armor assisting them not from mutants, but people. One had a medic kit.

"Don't hurt us!" a young man yelled.

"We just want to stop the bleeding!" another woman said, right before being shot with a paralyzer gun on the left side of her face.

"He's meant to die!" the MCS soldier said that had struck her. "Let him bleed."

"At least let us help the police officer," the man said.

Josh had called backup, trying to get to Charles between all the chaos that ensued around him. People were trying to get to Charles to protect him and others to kill him, or at least stop him. Some were after Kimberly. His partner sat on the ground, clinching his ankle.

"I'm okay," the cop muttered, pulling his gun and aiming it at the crowd. "Everyone stand back." He dropped the gun and winced in pain. Welts and bruising covered his skin wherever the snake-like thing touched him. All three scientists tried to protect the medic from harm as he made his way to the cop, all the while watching Charles. They knew in only minutes Kimberly would be back, and they didn't know what she was capable of when she returned from her paralyzed state.

Sven questioned why Charles wasn't being targeted with the paralyzer gun intended for mutants, but the crowd obstructed their aim. Making bystanders paralyzed might aid his getaway.

Sven hit the ground after being shoved in the back from the people fighting around him, banging his knee and an audible cracking sound followed.

Jesse lifted him up. "Time to take care of this once and for all. Stay behind me. You know I'm right."

"I didn't help you at the mutant attack just for you to get yourself killed." Sven moaned, clutching his knee. They both turned to see Adam inch closer to the chaos around Josh, Charles, and Kimberly. The ten minutes were almost up, and the paralyzer gun would have lost its effectiveness. Charles had already stabbed a few people with his knife, but was growing weaker as he continued to bleed.

"Adam isn't swift enough for this. It's me." Jesse weaved through the people, luckily not getting shot, drugged, or stabbed. Almost in arm's length of Kimberly, Sven panicked as he tried to hobble toward him. No one paid Sven any mind; he wasn't a threat in his condition.

Jesse reached for the knife that Charles dropped from his weakened hands, gripped the handle with all of his strength, and reached around Charles to stab Kimberly.

"Stop this, Jesse, and get back here," Sven spat, tension filling his body. *So bullheaded. The boy is going to give me a heart attack.*

"Get out of the way!" Josh shouted to Jesse as Kimberly motioned to take another grab at her father's arm after the paralyzer gun wore off. Kimberly missed and grabbed onto another opponent in her way, a scientist from Juniper Ridge. Her claws jabbed deep into his shoulder.

Blood sprayed as the man clutched onto his wound, howling in pain. Jesse lost his footing and fell backward, hitting the dirt right before three loud booms, and Kimberly plunged to the ground, the last motion, her reaching out for Charles' hand.

Charles cried, disoriented, his face alabaster white. He collapsed on the forest floor in a puddle of his own blood from his wrist wounds.

"Jesse!" Adam shouted after the boom, Sven right behind him.

"I'm fine." Jesse held up his hands, showing his body unharmed. Jesse's face fell when he saw the man bleeding everywhere. "I should have let Josh do his thing. Holy shit." Jesse took off his shirt and pressed it against the wound in the man's shoulder, but it was too deep and blood soaked through, dripping off the shirt's edges.

Sven realized he was holding his breath and let it out in one big swoosh. Placing his palm on his forehead, he shook his head.

It was finally over.

Most of Juniper Ridge doctors went into medic mode, helping the injured while the MCS stayed around the perimeter in look-out. People were departing while others were being bandaged up. An MCS utility vehicle moved in to take care of Kimberly, treating her as a mutant even though she had no contact with the virus. Jesse and Adam were urging him to get medical attention for his knee, but he insisted on staying and watching, needing proof that it was truly over.

Sven reached out his hand to shake Josh's. "Thank you." Josh walk away when Sven stopped him.

"Were you really captured or was that just a part of your story?"

Josh smiled, pausing before speaking. "I guess it doesn't matter now that you know. I was captured and released to return home to check on Jill after hearing of Daniel's death. They needed an overseer to make sure the new Juniper Ridge didn't break any laws, and when we found out there was a major drug ring with the serum, they had me look into that as well." Josh walked toward the ambulance. "I need to check on my partner."

When they were about ready to move Charles, Sven stopped them in a rush. "We need that vial," he said. The MCS equipped with gloves reached into his pocket and retrieved the vial, handing it to Sven to analyze at Juniper Ridge.

Sven gripped it tightly, never letting go.

# CHAPTER THIRTY-SIX

Adam and Jesse sat on either side of Sven, sitting in the front row of the church. Adam's family of four took up the right end of the pew while Jesse sat with Jennifer and Lily on his left. An arrangement of orchids stood next to Hannah's vibrant yellow urn. Sven thought of how the color represented the brightness that she had in his life, and kneaded his hands together in his lap, not knowing where to put them. She always loved when the orchids bloomed. When they weren't such a rarity, Sven liked to surprise her with the flowers just because he wanted to. Sven knew she would approve.

Sven tucked his feet in a smidge as people walked through, glad that he had his Boneflex injection the day before on his knee. With an injection going all the way down to the bone, it heals a joint in minutes.

Blowing his nose on the Kleenex left at the end of the pew, he let the tears fall, the pain in his chest lightning. A few slipped out, and he covered his face with his hands, letting them escape, his whole body shaking. Adam squeezed his left shoulder, and somehow that helped his breathing, but he continued to cry. That squeeze was Hannah, letting him know it was okay to let go.

"I love you, Hannah," he whispered. "There will come a day when I see you again. I have to stay here for now."

Jesse moved over and someone crying reached out to grab Sven's hand and took his place. Sven opened his eyes to see Nathan sitting next to him, and they cried together.

Sven apologized for everything, saying, "I'm sorry. I love you, Nathan."

"I love you, too."

Once Sven's eyes cleared, he flipped around to see rows of people that loved Hannah and that loved him. Neighbors, friends, and colleagues from Juniper Ridge sat with downcast eyes and murmured to each other.

*And I was afraid of being alone.*

He didn't have the strength to go up to the podium, but sat back and listened to all the stories of how Hannah had changed everyone's lives. Stories of when she babysat kids, visited people in the hospital, and brought the elderly medications and cared for them. *She deserves her place in heaven, Sven thought. How could I have taken that away from her? I was so lucky to have loved her.*

After the service, Nathan stayed right by his side as he made his way to the back. Jesse, Jennifer, and Lily fought through the crowd, and Lily reached out to him without saying a word, swallowing him in a hug.

"How long are you in town for?" asked Sven.

"The weekend," she said, eyes streaked with tears. Lily blew her nose on a tissue from her pocket and held onto it.

"Thank you for coming." She smiled and nodded.

"You remember Jennifer from the hospital?" Jesse introduced Jennifer, reaching down to hold her hand.

Jennifer smiled and looked down at her feet. "It was a beautiful service."

"What did you do with Max?" asked Jesse.

"My neighbor is dog-sitting. Sometimes I think Max is smarter than me. At least I don't have to be in that house all by myself."

"Max is lucky to have you," said Lily.

"Imagine having Williams as an owner." Jesse shuttered.

"Oh, I think he took care of him pretty well." Sven thought of how Charles had doted on his dog. The look in Charles' eyes when he spoke of his daughter was full of love, even if he was trying to hide it from Sven. With all his faults, there was a glimmer of goodness.

"About how I was acting when we were taking down Charles, I'm sorry. I didn't mean to get in the way. If I would have followed the plan, Peter Dawson might still be alive." Jesse's face flushed while Jennifer rubbed his back.

"Who?" asked Sven.

"The man that the girl accidentally grabbed reaching for Williams. He worked at the Ridge with us. God, I think it was his first year." Jesse shook his head. "If I would have let Josh take the shot and got out of the damn way..."

Sven hadn't seen Jesse this upset in a long while. "It wasn't your fault, Jesse. We'll talk about it later. I'm tired. There's so much today." Sven's eyes grew downcast as he eyed the swarm of people.

"I'm sorry. I shouldn't be talking about this now. We're celebrating Hannah's life today."

"We can go," said Nathan. "I'm sure the church will take care of all of this and I can come by later to help."

"Almost," Sven said right before Adam found him.

After a quick hug, Adam said, "I'm proud of you. If you need anything, you make sure to give me a call, okay?"

Sven nodded right before he heard running. He looked down to see Camille next to him, arms open wide. Her blonde ringlets tied in a yellow bow matched her dress. Squatting down to her level, she jumped into his arms. Sven laughed and cried, embracing the child.

"I like your dress," he told her.

"Thank you." She narrowed her eyes at the attendees wearing black. "I guess I'm the only one here that knows yellow was Hannah's favorite color."

"Camille," Adam scolded.

Sven shook his head and laughed. The innocence of a child. "It's okay," said Sven, tapping her on the nose. "She's right."

"Where's Mommy?" asked Adam. Camille pointed to the lady's room.

Sven's shoulders relaxed as he yawned.

"We'll take care of all of this. You go home and rest," said Adam.

"I wouldn't mind a nap. I'll see you two on Monday? We can start analyzing that concentrated serum and see what Charles really had in that vial."

"I'm taking Monday off," said Adam. Jesse jumped back while Sven rubbed his chin in concern. "Nothing bad." Adam waved his hands in front of them with a smile. "Camille has a karate tournament on Monday and I need to be there. I'm sure you two can handle it for one day."

Camille smiled up at her father. "I'm going to kick ass."

Adam groaned while Sven patted her on the head. "Well, good luck. Thanks again for coming."

It felt like a long walk to the front to grab the urn. "Come on, Hannah. It's time we go home."

—·—

# ACKNOWLEDGEMENTS

As I sit here at my desk in my fingerless Edgar Allen Poe gloves and hot cup of coffee, I don't even know where to begin. Many people have helped me with this project at every step.

First of all, I would like to thank my writing coach Veronica Jorden from First Book Coaching for not only reading and critiquing, but being my brainstorming anchor. She became as excited as I was when something clicked and encouraged me when I needed it the most. I learned a lot from you, Veronica!

Thank you to my beta readers. This was Sara's second beta read for me, and her mad beta skills and attention to detail do not go unnoticed. Noah had encouraging words and great tips to make this book the best that it could be.

For all of the other writers that have helped me with advice, many that I have met at book signings, especially Kelly Romo, for answering all my questions.

Thank you to my best friend Rachel for always supporting me and asking, "what's happening in the book today?"

Thank you to my boyfriend, Peter, who listened to me talk about my fictional world and characters like I just saw them.

My friend and coffee buddy, J.J., for supporting me through all the ups and downs.

Last, but not least, thank you to all the readers out there who have taken the time to jump into the future at Panacea. Just remember, always have a weapon close.

—·—

# ABOUT THE AUTHOR

R uth A. Milligan lives in the Pacific Northwest and loves curling up with a hot cup of coffee and submerges herself in a book.

When she's not reading or writing, she enjoys hockey games, concerts, and trips to the beach.

For updates of upcoming books, visit her website: ruthami lligan.com where you can sign up for her newsletter or join her author page on Facebook.